Sir Alan Herbert was born in 189
and Oxford. Having achieved a f
joined the Royal Navy and serv
France during the First World War. He was called to the Bar in 1918, and went on to become a Member of Parliament for Oxford University from 1935 to 1950.

Throughout his life A P Herbert was a prolific writer, delighting his many readers with his witty observations and social satires in the columns of *Punch*. He was the creator of a host of colourful characters – notably Topsy, Albert Haddock and Mr Honeybubble – and wrote novels, poems, musicals, essays, sketches and articles. He was also a tireless campaigner for reform, a denouncer of injustice and a dedicated conserver of the Thames.

By the time of his death in 1971, he had gained a considerable following and was highly regarded in literary circles. J M Barrie, Hilaire Belloc, Rudyard Kipling and John Galsworthy all delighted in his work, and H G Wells applauded him saying, 'You are the greatest of great men. You can raise delightful laughter and that is the only sort of writing that has real power over people like me.'

BY THE SAME AUTHOR
ALL PUBLISHED BY HOUSE OF STRATUS

A.P.H. His Life and Times
General Cargo
Honeybubble & Co.
The House by the River
Light Articles Only
Look Back and Laugh
Made For Man
Mild and Bitter
More Uncommon Law
Number Nine
The Old Flame
The Secret Battle
Sip! Swallow!
The Thames
Topsy, MP
Topsy Turvy
Trials of Topsy
Uncommon Law
The Water Gipsies
What a Word!

THE MAN ABOUT TOWN

A P HERBERT

HOUSE OF STRATUS

First published in 1923
Copyright © Teresa Elizabeth Perkins and Jocalyn Herbert

All rights reserved. No part of this publication may be reproduced, stored in a retrieval system, or transmitted, in any form, or by any means (electronic, mechanical, photocopying, recording, or otherwise), without the prior permission of the publisher. Any person who does any unauthorised act in relation to this publication may be liable to criminal prosecution and civil claims for damages.

The right of A P Herbert to be identified as the author of this work has been asserted.

This edition published in 2001 by House of Stratus, an imprint of Stratus Holdings plc, 24c Old Burlington Street, London, W1X 1RL, UK. Also at: Suite 210, 1270 Avenue of the Americas, New York, NY 10020, USA.

www.houseofstratus.com

Typeset, printed and bound by House of Stratus.

A catalogue record for this book is available from the British Library and the Library of Congress.

ISBN 1-84232-592-2

This book is sold subject to the condition that it shall not be lent, resold, hired out, or otherwise circulated without the publisher's express prior consent in any form of binding, or cover, other than the original as herein published and without a similar condition being imposed on any subsequent purchaser, or bona fide possessor.

This is a fictional work and all characters are drawn from the author's imagination. Any resemblances or similarities to persons either living or dead are entirely coincidental. This book contains opinions which, since the time of writing, have acquired racist connotations that some people may find offensive.

These Papers appeared originally in the pages of *Punch*, with the exception of two, one of which was printed in the New York *Life*, the other being based on some original MSS in the possession of the Port of London Authority and a copy of *Land and Water* at the British Museum. I wish to thank the proprietors of *Punch* and *Life*, and the executors of *Land and Water* for their courtesy and public spirit in permitting me to give these Studies to the world in this form.

APH

DEDICATION

DEAR SIR OWEN SEAMAN,
 It was your fate to read these Works in manuscript: and I suspect that you have also read them in print. You are therefore that rare friend to the author, a man who has read him twice, and still is kind. I hope there may be others as forbearing, and I venture with respect and gratitude to present them to you again. Not that I expect you to read them a third time; but if, here and there, they do get a Third Reading, I know how much they will owe to your care and guidance on the Committee stage.
  Yours sincerely,
   A P HERBERT.

HAMMERSMITH,
 30th *August* 1923.

CONTENTS

THE MAN ABOUT TOWN

SIXPENNY DIPS	3
TURKISH DELIGHT	8
THE HANDS OF DESTINY	14
FOREIGN FOOD	19
FOREIGN RELATIONS	24
A PLEASANT SUNDAY EVENING	29
THE ANNUAL DINNER	34
FINANCE	40
CHARITY	45
CLUB LIFE	51
THE PHARISEES	57
SECRET GOLFING	63
BOHEMIA	68
TATTERSALL'S	73
ART	78
A HOT-BED	83
THE COURT THEATRE	89
THE FIRST NIGHT	94
THE PERILS OF POLITENESS	100
THE PARLIAMENT OF MOTHERS	105
LE BOXE	110
A FEW SAMPLES	115

NEVER AGAIN
OR, PEOPLE I DON'T PLAY GOLF WITH TWICE

1.	JENKINS	123
2.	SPICER	127
3.	SIMPSON	131
4.	WINTHROP	135
5.	RICKWOOD	139
6.	COLLINS	144
7.	POSTSCRIPT	149

MARINERS OF ENGLAND

1.	THE SHARK	157
2.	THE WRECKERS	162
3.	THE LOBSTER	167

ETCETERA

A "RAG"	175
PIN-DROPS	179
THE BLUE FAIRY-BOOK	184
BINGO	187
THE ADVOWSONEER	191
FRANÇOIS	195
A LITTLE RIOT	199
THE LITTLE HORSE	203
CORAL ISLAND	208
THE BATTLE OF THE STEPS	219

THE MAN ABOUT TOWN

SIXPENNY DIPS

Recently I took George Rowland to the Dome of Dance with a lady friend of his. They are both West End dancing experts, and the admired of Nero's and the Nouveau Riche.

Now the Dome of Dance is almost wildly respectable. It is evacuated respectably at midnight, and provides no refreshment more sinister than a Sundae. But in George's view anything west of Earl's Court is practically in the East End; and he had pictured the Dome as a very low haunt indeed, peopled principally by Russians and other criminals, and surrounded by well-equipped opium dens, to which, after a few rather passionate dances, the fast young aristocrat is lured by a decoy-girl, and there drugged, robbed, and ultimately destroyed.

When we entered the place he stood amazed. The dancing was in full swing, and a number of suburban ladies and gentlemen were revolving assiduously round a large block of ice. The ice stood in a sort of tray in the centre of the room and was decorated with coloured lights and ferns. The dancers wore an expression of pain, sorrow, or remorse – except a few who sidled furtively along the rails, and these merely looked desperately unhappy. The band was playing "Rubenstein's Melody in F" as a one-step. They looked very happy indeed, and one of them sang through a megaphone, "Do'an't tell *me* to go to Dix-ee."

George was fascinated by the ice.

"What's that in the middle?" he asked.

"Ice," I said.

"Good Lord! What's it for?"

"Cooling the passions," I said. "You get a tough crowd here."

"Ah!" said George, brightening up.

"Well, take the floor, you two." I said, adding with a touch of bravado. "I may have a Sixpenny Dip."

"A *what*?"

"A Sixpenny Dip – a dancing partner – one of the instructresses, you know."

George was shocked. "Do you mean to say you can *hire* a partner here?" he said.

"Yes. They sit in that pen. The men are in the other one – over there. But a man costs ninepence."

"Good *Lord!*" said George. "But that's *disgusting*. No wonder you get a tough crowd. They can't dance, though. Come on, Daphne."

Daphne and George flung themselves into the solemn crowd with derisive movements of the shoulders. Heading swiftly for the block of ice they executed with great *bravura* the very latest step. The name of it escapes me, but George tells me it has taken Nero's by storm and broken many hearts at the Nouveau Riche.

The step looked simple. First George stood in one place, rotating rapidly on one heel, while Daphne ran round him on one toe, the other foot being raised in such a manner as to make it clear that she was wearing a very costly petticoat. Then George stood in another place, rotating rapidly on the other heel, and Daphne ran or was whirled all round him, with the other foot raised; and there was no doubt at all that she was still wearing a petticoat.

When they had done this two or three times there emerged from behind the block of ice a man in full evening dress, with a face like an exceedingly analytical novelist. He tapped George on the shoulder and (as I afterwards heard) said, "Sorry, sir, but we don't allow that here. This is not the West End… "

George came scowling off the floor, but I fled. Rather than run the risk of being seen by the Master of Ceremonies embracing the deplorable Daphne, I would dance with dips and nothing but dips.

I bought six tickets and stood sheepishly with some other desperadoes near the pen.

In theory the thing is easy; the ladies sit in the pen during the interval between dances, and you wait at hand till the music starts, deciding in your own mind, but, of course, without staring, which will be the best sixpenny-worth. There were about twelve, and I decided that seven of them were much the best. The music started, and I waited just a moment – not shy, of course, but not wishing to be too forward, you know. During that moment all my seven selections departed swiftly into the arms of stronger men. However, the other five looked pleasant and kindly enough in their neat uniforms. I whispered boldly (to myself), "May I have this, please?" and advanced like a wolf on the fold.

Then my tie wanted straightening; and when I had put it right there remained but one ewe lamb in the pen. She looked pleasant and kindly enough in her neat uniform; at the same time, out of the whole twelve, I should scarcely have put her higher than, say, twelfth. However...

I approached and said in a manly voice, "Oh – er!"

The next thing I knew we were cannoning into the ice. The ice reminded me of George's comments on the "dip" system, and I felt desperately wicked.

While we danced, we conversed; and while we conversed I began to feel less wicked.

Anyone who has ever danced with a not very talkative leg-of-mutton will appreciate my new sensations.

I was sorry for the girl. I said, "Not much of a life this, is it?"

"It is and it isn't," she said.

We danced round the room, while I thought this out.

Then I said, "Tiring life, I expect?"

She said, "In a way – but there it is."
We danced round the room again.
Then I said," You get a queer lot of partners, I expect?" and trod heavily on her toe.
"Some's better than others," she said.
Having found out the secrets of her life in this way I sought to impart a lighter tone to our conversation.
We passed close to the ice.
"Funny – that," I said.
"Funny?"
"The ice."
"Yes, it's naice, isn't it?" said she. "The ferns and that."
"Ought to be a salmon on the top," I said brightly.
"Pretty, wouldn't it?" she said gravely.
Then the music stopped. She held out her hand. I clasped it warmly, pleased by this evidence of human feeling.
She said, with no great emotion, "The ticket, please."
I unclasped hastily, and she fled back to the fold, clasping the ticket.
For the next dance, made bold by experience, I secured a charming partner – easily the eleventh best. She seemed full of life; and this was a special dance. The band played an air from *Tannhäuser* as a waltz. The ordinary lights were lowered, and from the balcony great beams of coloured light were shot across the gloom, making the dancers green and blue and heliotrope in turn. It was a very passionate scene.
Under the spell of the music and the lights and the voluptuous rhythm of the dance we talked.
I said, "Not much of a life, this – is it?"
She said, "It is and it isn't." And suddenly her face turned a livid green, like an old cheese.
I whispered, "Tiring life, I expect?"
"In a way," she said. "But there it is."
I looked into her eyes, and her face went a bright blue. I looked across the wide floor and saw a multitude of men and

women, some green, some blue, but all enchanted. I saw George. George was behaving himself now. But he had gone green.

I said, "You get a queer lot of partners, I expect?"

She turned heliotrope. I felt that I had gone too far.

Controlling herself, she said, "Some's better than others."

I saw then that there was a Standard Conversation for Dips, which I was following perhaps too closely for this romantic dance. The music, the lights, the shadowy spaces, the coloured women, the ice – A thrill ran through me.

I murmured passionately, "I like you best heliotrope."

She said, "I think the mauve's naicer."

The music stopped. I gave her a ticket, though it seemed sacrilege. Then I gave her my four remaining tickets. For, as she quaintly said, she got a commission on each, dance or no.

A commission on the aching hearts of men! Ah me!

"Well, you've been going it!" said George. "This *is* a place!"

"Ha!" said I, the unrepentant libertine.

"Oh, George," said Daphne piteously, "*do* let me have a Ninepenny Dip!"

TURKISH DELIGHT

"I will *not* have a Turkish Bath," I said for the seventh time.

"Do you good," said George. "You're run down."

"It is now 11 a.m. Only three hours ago I carefully washed and dressed myself. Rather than do it all over again I will willingly remain run down. I will *not* – "

"This is the place," said George.

A Turkish Bath, I have often heard, eases the mind. This is done by gradually converting a man into a mere body.

First they took my hat and coat away.

Then a man took my watch and jewels and locked them in a drawer.

Then another man took my boots off and hid them.

Then, defenceless, I was driven into the *frigidarium* and told to take my clothes off.

Then a man took my divine soul and locked it in a locker.

And finally, reduced to the condition of a beast of the field, I was goaded gently into the *tepidarium*. I had a feeling that the right way to enter the *tepidarium* would be on all-fours. (Few men, I believe, at this stage offer any further resistance.)

George had provided me with a little booklet, *Hints to Bathers*, to which I clung desperately.

"The domed *tepidarium*," I read, "is kept at a temperature of 110 degrees. It is lined with white marble. Here the bather pours some tepid water over the head, and rests some five or ten minutes before passing into either of the hotter rooms, where he awaits the free outburst of perspiration."

"You *must sweat*, you see," said George; "otherwise it's bad for you."

"Very well," I said, and we sat down.

It was pleasantly warm in the *tepidarium* – warm and quiet, though a trifle gloomy. No sound broke the stillness, and only one other person was present – an exceedingly fat man, quite naked, reading *The Westminster Gazette*. Exactly what there is that is funny in a fat man with no clothes on reading *The Westminster Gazette* I can't say, but I maintain that it is funny. I began to giggle. A low mind? Doubtless. But I giggled, terribly.

"Are you sweating?" said George sternly.

"Frankly – no."

In the excitement of giggling I had forgotten to sweat.

"Then come in here."

George pulled aside a heavy curtain, hot to the touch, and revealed a small room.[1] I recoiled in horror.

In the room were two bodies.

It was very sad. They lay in deckchairs, one a young man, but large and fleshy; the other very old, with very white hair and a very red face So still, so shiny, it was odd to think that but a few hours back they too had briskly walked this London of ours and paid their money at the door; till the very last, perhaps, they had read those saturated rags upon the floor, which once had been evening papers. And now…

Yet, happy ones, at least they had accomplished the Great Sweat…

Pondering this, I sat down slowly on a red seat, and stood up again very quickly. The seat was red-hot.

"I don't like this," I said.

"Oh, this is nothing," said George. "This is only about 140. Come in here. This is 180." And he disappeared behind another curtain.

I sat down gingerly and read my book.

"At first," I read, "not seldom the bather on commencing the bath fails to perspire. In this case he should be removed from the chamber in ten minutes, have warm water poured over him, be well shampooed and returned to the hot chamber."

It seemed to me that ten minutes was up. I removed my body from the *sudarium* and replaced it in the *tepidarium*. Then I poured warm water over it and sat down. The fat man had disappeared. It was quiet and peaceful. I admired the marble lining. I felt just a little Byzantine. I went to sleep.

I woke with a guilty sensation, vaguely conscious of some duty neglected.

I peeped into the first *sudarium*. It was empty. The bodies had been removed.

I went through and peeped into the second room. A wave of heat – hotter heat than ever – struck me in the face. There lay the bodies. There too lay George and the fat man – all still, all shiny. The fat man's *Westminster Gazette* had become a pulp. It was horribly hot. The heat, the silence, the prostrate bodies, the sense of doom – it was as if one had walked into the last scene of an Elizabethan tragedy.

I walked once round the room, like a cat on hot bricks. Then I felt that I must either speak or scream.

"I don't like this," I said.

A sort of ripple of protest passed over the bodies. George opened an outraged eye and immediately closed it again. I went back into the *tepidarium*.

Hours passed.

George tottered out. The fat man tottered out, still clutching a sodden mass of printed paper, and, silent, inflexible, passed into the third chamber.

"Are you sweating?" said George.

"Practically," I said.

"Not good enough," said he. "*Come in here.*"

He led the way into the Russian Steam Bath, or Asphyxiating Cell, full of damp heat, and horrible.

"This'll do the trick," said George, and turned on a tap. Steam emerged from everywhere, hissing. I saw that I was to be scalded to death.

"I don't like this," I said; and I rushed out into the *tepidarium.* George followed a little later.

"Dash it," he said, "you *must sweat.* Otherwise it's fatal."

"Kismet!" I replied. "I hope I am prepared to meet my fate like a gentleman, but rather than sweat in a place like that I will never sweat again."

"*Come in here,*" said George, and entered the third chamber – a mere 200 degrees. A blast of heat smote me at the door.

"I don't like this," I said.

"This is nothing," said George, composing himself comfortably on a couch. "The next one's 250."

I cautiously advanced a nose into the fourth room, where the heat was so hot that obviously no human being could live in it for ten minutes. There lay the fat man, sweating assiduously, and by now scarcely to be described as fat.

I went back to the *tepidarium.*

Days passed. The two other men stole silently across to the third room. The attendant vanished. I was alone.

I rose and ran rapidly round the *tepidarium* – round and round, knees up, chest out – several times. Then I sat down.

George came out with the fat man, by now a mere skeleton.

"That's better," he said. "You're sweating beautifully."

"Thanks, old man," I said with modest pride. "What next?"

George clapped his hands. "Shampoo – best of all."

Three men of great physical strength appeared, arrayed like torturers in scarlet loincloths. They laid our bodies on marble slabs, like so many salmon or joints of beef, and a hideous scene began.

My man was, if anything, more powerful than the others. Resistance was hopeless. He rubbed me brutally with a camel's-hair glove.[2] He covered me with soap. He washed me with a wisp of the Mecca palm.[3] He picked up an arm here or a leg there, and soaped it, or rubbed the skin off it, or simply hit it. He threw buckets of water over me. He turned me upside down and gave me three or four resounding slaps over the liver, followed by a rhythmical but murderous tattoo with his clenched fists in the same quarter. Once or twice I struggled to rise, but "Stay as you are," he muttered grimly, and I stayed. Finally, he allowed me to sit up, covered my head with lather and dashed a great quantity of water in my face.

"Now take a shower," he said.

I stood up feebly. I had the soap in my eyes; and I felt as a small child must feel when it is bathed for the first time by a strange and uncongenial aunt. Few men are quite at their best when they are naked and have the soap in their eyes; and I was now as wax in the man's hands.

He led me under a boiling shower, which immediately became very, very cold. He stood me in a corner and turned a fire-hose on me. Then he led me to the edge of an icy plunge-bath and looked at me.

I looked at him, incredulous. "Can it be possible," I thought, "that after all I have been through I am now expected to *dive* into a *cold* bath?"

His eye said "It's not *necessary* – but, of course, no gentleman – "

No man looks at me twice in that way.

"Curse you!" I muttered, and dived.

The Man About Town

In the *frigidarium* George was having a cocktail. "Topping, isn't it?" he said. "Does you a world of good." The fat man was weighing himself with one hand and drinking sherry with the other. He looked pleased.

Later, at the Club, I saw him lunching. He lunched extremely well, chiefly on Burgundy and steak-and-kidney pudding. His companion chaffed him on his appetite.

"Oh, well," he said, "I deserve a good lunch. I lost five pounds this morning. Waiter, I'll have a large glass of port!"

1 *Sudarium*, or sweat-place.
2 The *kheesah* of India.
3 Or *lyf*.

THE HANDS OF DESTINY

"It's all very depressing," said George, throwing down the paper in disgust, "I shall go and have a manicure."

It was after luncheon at the Club. All about us, men of evident affluence reclined in leather chairs and, sadly consuming coffee and cigars, discussed in low tones the gloomy condition of the world.

"There's no way out that I can see," said a large man. "Bring me a brandy, waiter."

"It's a black look-out, certainly," said his companion. "I'll have a small port."

"True," said I to George; "but will a manicure improve it all?"

"Whenever I'm depressed," he said, "I go to Thomas'. There's a girl there –" and George assumed an extremely dreamy expression. "Where do you go?" he inquired.

"I don't," I said. "I mean I don't go to Thomas'. I go to different places – Rupert's, and Stanley's, and – and so on."

"I don't know them," said George.

"No?"

"You ought to stick to the same place," said George, studying his immaculate fingers. "Can't expect to have your hands nice otherwise. Come on, I'll take you there." And he jumped up with a much more optimistic air.

"I don't really think I want –" I began.

"Oh, yes, you do. When was your last?"

"My last?" said I, plunging my hands into my pockets. "Well, of course the Election upset things a good deal. I really forget – "

"Oh, come *on*! Dora's a peach."

"But I don't *know* Dora."

By this time George had shattered the spell of quietness in the room, and several large men rose up and, muttering something about "the office," shambled out of the door.

George is very strong-willed. "Anyhow, you can have your hair cut," he said as we walked up Piccadilly.

"It was cut last week."

"Well, anyway – " said George; and suddenly we were in the shop.

Thomas' is a kind of small mosque, all tiles and Moorish arches, and crudely coloured glass through which the sun comes but dimly; and small partitioned shrines are set along the walls.

"Funny place, isn't it?" said George. "Rather romantic, I always think. Oriental and all that."

"It *is* funny," I said. "And when one thinks how seldom they shave in the East and how rarely a Moor has his hair cut, it's funnier still."

But the high-priest was upon us, bowing low.

"Two manicures," said George, as easily as if he had said "Two melons."

"Two manicures – suttinly, Sir," said the high-priest, bowing, and cried into a speaking-tube the words, "Next two manicures *up*, please," and from far below were heard the words, "Next two manicures – *right*."

And we waited under the vaulted dome...

The rustle of silk was heard.

At this point, in a clear voice, I heard myself saying, "I should like a hair-cut."

"Come this way, Sir," said the high-priest; and before George could open his mouth I had escaped into a secure shrine in the male quarters, entirely surrounded by hair-oil and looking-glass.

To contemplate one's profile from every possible angle without physical effort is a rare and soothing experience to the least handsome among us; and the high-priest left me to enjoy this for some time.

Then came a priest, not quite so high, and said in a very courtly way, "Do you wish the hair cut short? Or perhaps a trim about the back and sides?"

"I don't want it cut any *shorter*," I said miserably. "It was cut last week. The fact is – "

"Shampoo, face massage, radio – ?"

"A shampoo," I said eagerly. "I couldn't think of the word."

"Suttinly, Sir. Wet or dry?"

"I forget," said I. "Which is which?"

"If-you-have-a-dry," he answered rapidly, "I-shall-first-open-the-pores-of-the-scalp-with-a-hot-towel-bound-round-the-head; then-with-a-preparation-of-oil-and – "

"Wet," I murmured desperately – "wet."

For sheer brutality give me a really expensive wet shampoo. The priest swathed me in suffocating towels, took firm hold of the nape of the neck, forcibly thrust the nose into a basin, turned a powerful hose of boiling water on the crown, vigorously pummelled the scalp, shouted in the ear, "Would you like it *cold*?" and, while the mouth was still spluttering "No," petrified the whole body with a murderous jet of iced water. He then tightly twisted a towel round the temples and by sharply jerking back the head attempted to dislocate the spine. Foiled there, he shook the head violently from side to side so as to detach it from the trunk. He then pressed a switch, tore out most of the surviving hairs with a revolving brush, scratched fiercely among the roots, and said, "The hair's very thin, Sir."

"I shouldn't wonder," I gasped.

"And the next, Sir?" he snapped. "Face massage, radio – "

"I think we'll leave the face as it is," I ventured. For at this point I imagined myself stealing out of the shop and abandoning George forever.

The priest bowed. "The young lady is waiting for the hands," he said, not without menace.

"The *hands?*" I faltered. "Oh, yes, of course – the hands"; and, taking out one of the hands, I examined it dispassionately "As a matter of fact – "

"*This* way, please," said the priest firmly.

By the discreditable exercise of some sort of psychic power I was now wafted swiftly to a row of shrines in a remote corner, more commodious and secluded than the others. In one of them was George and a young lady, looking exceedingly romantic. In three others also there were men whose faces were vaguely familiar. Where had I seen them? At the Office – the Underground – the Club?

At the Club – lunchtime.

I entered my shrine, feeling that in ten minutes I should be engaged to be married.

The young lady was friendly, pleasant, but discreet. She took one of the hands and laid it out on a cushion.

"I've been doing a good deal of manual labour," I said hastily. "Gardening and carpentering, and – "

"Very int'resting work, of *course*," she said reproachfully, "but absolutely *fatal* for the hands. Still, they're not so bad," she added kindly.

I breathed again.

She worked quickly. A terrifying trayful of files, knives, scissors, nippers, tin-openers, tweezers, and metal-polishers stood at her side, and, seizing the hand, she put it through a ruthless course of pruning, paring, filing, and slicing. In five minutes but few traces of the original hand remained.

However, I must say that after the shampoo it was a comparatively restful, though expensive, process; and this no doubt explains the origin and purpose of the shampoo.

Meanwhile we talked.

She said she liked manicuring more than hair-dressing, though she used to do both, and, of course, in a way she had been in the business since she was eight, and that was only thirteen years ago, though you might not think it, because her father and mother were both in the hairdressing, and her sisters too, and they'd been brought up hearing nothing else since they were quite tiny, and what with everyone talking "shop" night and day, of course one did get a bit sick of it – anyone would – all the same…

The idea of a happy childhood marred only by too much hairdressers' "shop" in the home moved me profoundly.

"Are you Dora?" I asked.

"No," she said. "Dora's farther along. She's going to be married."

"A dark young man? Small moustache? Name of George?"

"That's the one."

"Funny," I mused. "He never told me – "

"P'r'aps he doesn't know," she said darkly, and dropped the hand in a bowl of hot water to soak. "Now the other one, please," she commanded.

"I – I don't think I've time to have the other one done," I said nervously, looking at my watch. "Not now. One day next week, perhaps."

"Men *are* funny," she remarked reflectively. "That's what my husband used to say."

"Oh, well," I said brightly, "I mustn't imitate *him*, must I?" and I fearlessly produced the hand.

She picked it up and filed it thoughtfully with a long, romantic-looking file.

"That's just what *he* did," she said.

FOREIGN FOOD

George Rowland is one of those restless people who are always looking for new places at which to lunch; and there is always one place which, for about six weeks, is so much the most glorious of all the eating-houses of London that he can scarcely bring himself to take food under any other roof. The pity is that these enthusiasts can never eat at their Elysia alone. True, if George asks you to lunch, he will name *The Rakes' Club* or *Stephen's*, but at the last moment he invariably rings up and tells you to make it the Russian Café, or the Czecho-Slovakian Restaurant, or the *Au Chapeau de ma Tante*, or the *Sombrero Bueno*, or whatever is the foreign favourite of the moment. Indeed I have often felt for him at breakfast-time, when he must make shift with common English food.

At present one of the Chinese restaurants heads the list – the one in Blue Street, no other.

"This is the only one in London where you can get Noodles done properly," he explained, as he ushered me, with Daphne, into the place.

Somehow I had expected a more exotic atmosphere. The room had much the aspect of an ordinary restaurant, but for a tropical palm which stood on the hat-stand in a small pot, the man at the door who looked like a stage Chinaman in *mufti*, and a waiter who was like one of the less pleasant natives of the island of Malta. As to the scattered members of the public, one might have been a Hindu, and the rest were Sydenhamians of the purest extraction. No one was using chopsticks.

"I come here nearly every day," said George happily. "Now what will you have? I usually have Chop Suey myself, with a spot of rice."

Daphne was eagerly studying the menu, at the most expensive page.

"Oh, do let me have some Sai Foo Yin Wo!" she said.

"Let's see," said George;" I forget what that is."

"Stewed-Bird's-Nest-with-Minced-Chicken-and-Water-lily-root," she read.

"Sorry – you have to give half a day's notice for that sort of thing," said George.

"Well, what about Chun Pee Arp? That sounds delicious."

"Stewed-Whole-Duck-with-Tangerine flavour?" read George, looking a little blue. "Yes, that's nice; but you'll have to wait a long time. Try some of these," he suggested, dexterously turning to a cheaper page.

"I'll have some Chop Suey and rice," I said gallantly, giving Daphne a lead. "And perhaps half a jelly-fish and cucumber salad to follow – Jit Pee Cheng Gwar."

"I don't like the name," said Daphne. "I shall have some Fried-Fishcake-with-Vermicelli-and-Shredded-Pork-in-Gravy – Too Bow Yonk Pin Tong."

"All right," said George. "And I'll have some Stewed-Chicken-cut-in-cubes-with-White-Olive-Seaweed."

"Oo, I'm so hungry!" said Daphne. "What fun eating real Chinese food! I wish we had chopsticks."

Just then a stout man sat down opposite to us with a friend.

"Yes, I often come here," he said. "Makes a change, you know. Waiter!"

"Nothing like a change of diet, I always say," the other agreed.

"Yes, one gets sick of the same old chop day after day. *Waiter!*"

"That's it. You want variety."

"Makes a change coming to a place like this," said the stout man genially. "Ever been here before? WAITER!"

"Don't know that I have. I generally go to Porter's. They give you a nice cutlet and peas there."

"Cosy little place, Porter's. I go to Bream's. WAI-*ter!*"

"I don't like the service at Bream's."

"They give you a darned good chop and potatoes for tenpence. Where the hell's that waiter?" said the stout man with diminished geniality.

The waiter arrived, set my Chop Suey before me, together with a mountainous bowl of rice, and took our other orders.

"Now what's your fancy?" said the stout man. "You'd better have one of these old-fashioned chinese dishes. Hungry?"

"So-so," said the thin man, with his eye on the messy scrap-heap in my bowl.

"Well, what about some Pork? Fried-Bitter-Melon-with-Pork-in-Gravy; or some Soup-with-Swimming-Bladder-Pork-and-Awabi? How's that?"

"Don't know that I could tackle that. I've not much of an appetite, not reelly."

"Well, have some Noodle. That's light. Fried-Crispy-Noodle-with-Prawn-and Vegetables."

"All right," said the thin man.

"One-Fried-Crispy-Noodle-with-Prawn and all the rest of it, waiter. And I'll have some Chop Suey – no, I think I'll have some Dry Noodle – no, I won't; I'm feeling a bit peckish today. I believe I'll have a chop after all. A chop and a baked potato. And send out for two half-pints of beer."

"Very sorry, Sir, no chop," said the Maltese.

"No *chop!* D'you mean to tell me I can't have a *chop*? Is this a restaurant, or what?"

"No, Sir," said the man.

"Ask the manager to come here," said the stout man grimly. "And order that portion of Noodle at once."

There followed a long and heated altercation with the manager. Did the manager mean to tell him that, in a public restaurant not a quarter of a mile from Piccadilly Circus, it was impossible to provide a hungry man with an ordinary underdone *chop*? He did. The gentleman could have Suey, Noodle, Jelly-fish, Awabi, Fried Bitter Melon, or Bird's Nest, or even a poached egg, but not a chop.

"Well, I'm – " said the stout man. "I'll have a poached egg, then. And look sharp."

"By Gad!" he went on bitterly, "I'll never come here again. It's disgraceful. If anyone had told *me* that I couldn't get a *chop* in a restaurant in Blue Street – It isn't *sense*. After all, it isn't everybody who wants to eat these darned Oriental concoctions, not if he's hungry. Ah, here's your Noodle," he added hospitably. "Tell me how you like it."

The thin man delicately tasted his Noodle.

"Very tasty," he said, but with no marked enthusiasm.

"Makes a change, doesn't it?" said the other cheerfully.

Meanwhile, encouraged by the waiting Daphne and George, I was wading through my Chop-Suey-and-Rice. I had eaten, as I judged, about a cubic foot of rice, but the mountain looked as large as before. From the other bowl I had eaten, I estimated, a hundredweight of queer messy fragments, which might be bamboo-shoots or seaweed or bits of jelly-fish nests or anything else for all I knew. The bowl seemed as full as ever, and I felt unusually ill.

I now understand the impassivity and the frugality of the Oriental. For the effect of the tiniest quantity of Chinese food is to make you feel that you can never eat again; yet at the same time hunger still gnaws at your vitals. You feel at once as full and as empty as a balloon; and if anyone put you in the sun you could hardly fail to burst. This is why the Chinese do not become really lively till after dark.

When Daphne's fish, pork, and vermicelli, and George's chicken and seaweed arrived, I had laid down my fork; and I had done with eating for many days.

"You don't look well," said George.

"I'm not," I said. "But go on. Don't let me spoil your lunch."

Daphne looked nervously at the dish before her; then she looked at my face (over the eyes of which there had passed a glassy film); and then with envy at the stout man's plate.

"George," she said shyly, "would you mind *very* much if – if – if I had a poached egg instead?"

"By all means," said George with a certain relief. "In fact, I think I'll join you."

He turned to me. And the fat man turned to the thin man. And they both said, "Look here, would *you* like a poached egg?"

The thin man sighed; and I saw that over his eyes there had passed a glassy film. "Not *now*," he said sadly.

"Not this week," said I.

FOREIGN RELATIONS

The passion for things Russian had always something spiritual in it, and that was why it spread rapidly through all grades of society. It was only in 1913 that the apotheosis of CHALIAPIN was complete among the upper classes, but, by 1918, quick to absorb a new idea, the Labour Party had followed suit with the apotheosis of LENIN. And now it has reached George.

George has skipped over the artistic and political phases, and gone straight to the purely spiritual side of the Russian genius. In fact, the psychic.

Perhaps it was my fault, for introducing George to Baranoff. Personally, though I know that this is a bourgeois taste, I like the Russians for themselves. All Russians seem to me to be charming (except, of course, the hell-hounds who have remained in Russia), and my old friend Baranoff is a dear. Baranoff had often spoken to me of Balalaikin, "the great spirit," with whom from time to time he had communication but I had never paid much attention. Then George began to talk about Balalaikin.

One day I found him deep in a book on Ancient Egypt. "Balalaikin says I'm mixed up with AMENHOTEP?" he said casually. "Eighteenth Dynasty."

A few days later he was studying a History of Ancient Greece. "Balalaikin," he explained. "I asked him why it was I so often get depressed. He said I had a great trouble in Greece, in the third century BC. Previous incarnation, you understand."

"Oh course," I said. "I should like to meet this man."

Baranoff lives with Petroff, and we met in Baranoff's bedroom. A planchette-board stood on the table. Before the general company arrived they explained about Balalaikin. George was rather apologetic about me, and feared that my frivolity might frighten the spirit away.

"No matter," said Baranoff; "Balalaikin very jokey man. *Pravda*. True. Look at roof."

We looked at the ceiling, which was flaked and crumbling in a manner quite remarkable for a suburban lodging-house.

"Balalaikin do all that," said Baranoff. "In one night. *Pravda*."

"He very great spirit," he went on. "Very talented man. Eight years I was speaking with him with my friend Petroff. He was officer in Russian Navy, but killed first year of war. He live by Volga – "

"Did you know him?" I asked.

"No. Neither of us know him alive."

"Have you looked him up in the Russian Navy List – to see if he really existed?"

"In 1723," said Baranoff sadly, "there was Naval officer that name. In 1914 other incarnation – other name. Understand?"

"Of course," I said.

Just then several Russian ladies and gentlemen came in, and for some minutes they all talked at once with considerable animation. It has long been a theory of mine that there are very few Russians (in London) who really know the Russian language. At any rate, so long as they talk Russian, they can seldom make each other understand what it is they mean. Sure enough in this case a deadlock was reached at last, and Petroff made a long explanation in French.

Baranoff translated the French for me. He said: "One day we put hands on *table à trois pieds* and it *commence à tapper*. Balalaikin say he have very important information for us and he will dictate *hundred volumes*."

"What number are you at now?" I inquired.

"Fifty-seven. But he not go in order. One day he say, 'This is thirty-three.' Other day he say, 'This is seventeen.' He begin at sixty-five."

"I see," I said.

"Here is volume," said Baranoff, producing a large notebook and opening it at a page of presumably, *vers libre* in Russian manuscript. "Very beautiful Hindu poem," he said. "Time third century before Christ."

"But I thought it was Balalaikin's?"

"Balalaikin dictate, but Hindu in spirit. He great specialist of India that time. Petroff will read."

Petroff read out the Hindu poem in Russian, and I drank it in. George was sitting on the bed with a pretty girl called Olga Popova, talking volubly. She talked broken English and he replied in broken French. They seemed to understand each other perfectly. Meanwhile, we all drank Russian *tchai* and ate chocolate and acid drops.

Paper was placed under the planchette-board; there was a stir of excitement, and we all rose and exchanged our seats – except Olga and George.

Baranoff and Petroff placed their hands on the board. The spirit of Balalaikin was then asked to state the previous incarnations of the stranger – me.

Balalaikin hesitated, then made a little dash across the paper, and wrote rather doubtfully:

"*Nitckevo*," said Petroff, and they removed their hands.

"He is not ready yet," Baranoff explained. We drank more *tchai*. Petroff took one of the volumes over to Olga, but she was deep in conversation and took no notice of him, poor man. "Ah, *oui!*" said George volubly, and Olga laughed her jolly Russian laugh.

Meanwhile Baranoff showed me the music which Balalaikin had dictated for the Hindu love-song.

They put the question again. Balalaikin remained mute for several moments. A flake fell from the ceiling, as if in protest. Then he wrote, more decidedly:

"*Nitchevo,*" said Petroff, desisting.

Baranoff showed me photographs of some pieces of sculpture which had been sculped according to the instructions of Balalaikin.

"Very versatile man," I said.

"Great specialist of Art," said Baranoff solemnly. "*Pravda.*"

They tried again. Balalaikin, in a fury, ran right off the paper – into the *tchai*-tray. They turned the paper upside down and brought him back.

Pleased by this attention the spirit wrote rapidly a number of Russian words. We watched him, breathless.

He wrote: "*Egypt time of* SET-NEKHT."

This gave general satisfaction. It was agreed that I had an unusually Egyptian cast of countenance, and many looked at me with a new respect.

But Balalaikin had not finished. He went on: "*Greece, third century* BC; *Flanders, twelfth century.*'

"Yes, I see what he means," said Lydia Puzanova mysteriously. "I can just imagine you in Flanders."

Then Balalaikin wrote:

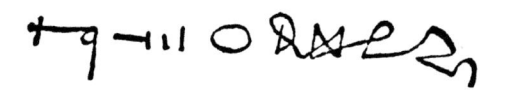

Baranoff gasped. "That means you have great mediumistic power," he said. "True."

I drained my *tchai* to the dregs.

After that Balalaikin expanded. Olga asked him:

"Why can I not sleep in London?"

Balalaikin pondered this for some time. Then he wrote in Russian:

"*1631 in Venice you lose your lover.*"

We all sighed in sympathy with Olga, and Petroff threw her an affectionate glance. So did George.

Olga herself was visibly impressed, and became very thoughtful.

Many other questions were put and answered, mostly with satisfaction, and all with a convincing grasp of the subject.

Lydia Puzanova asked, "Where is my friend Boris Malinin, whom I have not seen for seven years?"

Balalaikin made a series of excited rushes across the table, then, steadying himself, answered helpfully:

"*Seek in Caucasus.*"

"So that's where he is," said Lydia thoughtfully.

"Is he always right?" I asked.

"Eightee per cent," she answered sadly.

And now Balalaikin was tiring. George had arranged to see Olga home, and we prepared to go. But Baranoff asked me if I had no question to put.

"Don't think so," I said idly; but my eye fell on George. "Yes, ask him how soon George will be married – and how many children he'll have?"

Baranoff wrote down the question and handed it to Petroff.

Balalaikin wrote at a great pace, in good round English:

"*Very soon. Twenty-seven.*"

Olga Popova went home alone.

A PLEASANT SUNDAY EVENING

If any think that George Rowland is entirely devoid of intellect they wrong the boy. Devoted he may be to the material pleasures of the Wicked City, but, like the best of his type, he never forgets that mind and body must be developed together. Few weeks pass without his glancing through a book, and, if it should take his fancy, as like as not he will read through a whole review of the work in question in the pages of some newspaper. That done, no one will more fairly or eloquently appraise the merits of the author at dinner-parties and At Homes; while, if the author should be a friend or acquaintance, he will lose no time in securing the book from a lending library, cost what it may.

Passionately devoted to music, he cherishes most among his possessions the superb Handelian Gramophone, which stands in the lacquer cabinet, ready at any moment to fill his flat with the "Song of a Nightingale in the New Forest," the art of female violinists and comedians, or the Negro Melody[1] from *What's Yours?* Indeed, with such loyal support from our affluent young men, no artist or author has any longer an excuse for starving.

But perhaps, intellectually, his ruling interest is The Theatre. He never misses a First Performance, except perhaps those Tragedy matinées which clash with one of the more important speed tests for horses in the country. And he belongs to the Extinct Play Society, to a performance of which I accompanied him some time ago.

The Society for the Resuscitation of Extinct Plays, to give it its full title, serves an admirable purpose in providing our more intellectual citizens with something to do on Sunday evenings. It produces no plays which have been dead for a shorter period than three hundred years; but every play performed is a masterpiece. Thus, unless the rules are altered, three solid centuries will probably pass before *What's Yours?* is again staged in London. A solemn thought.

On this particular Sunday the play was Maxter's masterpiece, *Come, Fill the Cup*. A brief note of three thousand words in very small type on the back of the programme explained when it had died, and why. It said:

"*Come, Fill the Cup* was first acted in the Tithe Barn, Smithfield, in 1621. There were three performances. The October riots of that year deprived the dramatist of the full appreciation that his masterpiece deserved... It was revived in 1625, when once again misfortune dogged the piece, the theatre being razed to the ground by an intolerant mob during the second performance... The play has not been staged since the year 1633, when a single performance was given in the Cheesehill Opera House, at Aldgate. Two days later Samuel Maxter was burned alive. His genius," etc., etc.

The audience filed in modestly, not to say furtively – a refined audience, yet an audience English to the core; for nearly all the ladies wore Russian dresses almost entirely concealed by Spanish shawls, with shoes of some quaint Turkish design, and perhaps a simple Chinese ornament hanging from the throat; and they peered at each other in a suspicious manner through large American spectacles of tortoiseshell, or (in the Circles) horn.

The men all wore a "Tomorrow will be Monday" expression.

The lady who sat down next to me was dressed, roughly, as above; she had a pale but intellectual face, and an atmosphere of intense culture and refinement surrounded her. One felt that her very digestion must be a purely intellectual process. She looked at those about her with some hostility, and said with a sigh to her companion, "*What* a lot of highbrows!"

The lady in front of me was dressed differently, but in the same style. Her spectacles were easily the largest in the stalls; but then she had very large eyes. With these she studied the faces of all persons to right and left; then, turning slowly till she had a perfect view of George and myself, she carefully examined us through the spectacles; then she took the spectacles off and looked at us naked; then she said with a sigh to her companion, "*What* a lot of highbrows!"

People who were sitting elsewhere have told me since that their neighbours in every case made identically the same remark. I have for some time been seeking to probe the nature and habits of the highbrow, and I felt that at last I had discovered him. But what was George doing there!

George was examining the programme. "That's her," he said; "Rachel Gay – a topping girl. Awfully good actress too," he added (the highbrow influence again).

But even the charms of Rachel Gay seemed to me an insufficient reason for the presence of George in that company.

Before the First Act the Secretary of the Society appeared on the stage and said that the Society was dying; but with the aid of three hundred new members and generous donations of money it could easily be restored.

The play began. A refined hush fell upon the audience. In the dark the ladies secretly removed their spectacles.

The piece was nothing if not robust. The first scene was a tavern – *Stagger, Slutt, Pearl (a Pigwoman), Mistress Slowly, Nose, Prickle,* and *Dogg discovered* – all drunk. They sang a tipsy song, and *Prickle* (a strolling jester) banged *Pearl* on the head with a bladder. Then *Pearl* (a hideous, wrinkled, toothless hag) clapped a colander over *Prickle's* head. And how the audience laughed!

I wish I could reproduce some of the robust seventeenth-century dialogue, but one or two passages alone remain in the memory. For example:

> "*Pearl*. Peace, you foul roaring jade, you –
> "*Slowly*. 'Od's foot, thou mountain of grease. Ha!
> "*Prickle*. What, pig-face, thou!
> "*Pearl*. Peace, pumpkin. Ha!
> "*Nose*. Thou hog of Houndsditch!
> "*Pearl*. Do you sneer, dog's-head?
> "*Nose*. Thou slut!
> "*Pearl*. Thou snout!
>   (*They drink again.*)"

This passage, during which a great deal of robust bladder-banging and other horse-play went on, sent the audience into refined screams of laughter, and the lady next to me had a violent fit of coughing. It was really jolly to see all these cultured people entering with such spirit into the fun of the thing.

In the Interval we all trooped out and stared at each other with loathing in the *foyer*. George and I stood near a very tall and repellent man, who carried a kind of wand and had a permanent wave.

"I *like* this audience," he remarked loudly, surveying the crowd with satisfaction. "One doesn't feel *odd*."

Before the Second Act the Treasurer of the Society came on and said that the Society was in a bad way; but all that was needed was five or six hundred new members and a substantial sum of money. Next year, if it was still alive, the Society proposed to revive seven more extinct plays, including Sligger's masterpiece, *The Horse-Leech*. Then we all sat back and said what a shame it was the public wouldn't support really *good* stuff in these degenerate days...

George enjoyed it too, though the production had one flaw for him. The charming and accomplished Rachel was playing *Pearl, the Pig-woman*. "Rotten shame," said George.

In the next Act the plot was developed, in what direction I forget, if I ever discovered; but it had to do with unfaithful wives, wife-beating husbands, trollops, pigs, cupboards, mistaken identities, pickpockets, wenches, sluts, and baggages. And there was another arresting piece of dialogue:

"*Nose.* 'Tis no sweet vapour, Sir; it stinks.
"*Prickle.* Yes, I think it does stink, good snout.
"*Nose.* Nay, Sir, it does not stink neither, by thy leave.
"*Prickle.* Ay, by my leave it may stink."

Again the audience rose to the jolly drunken fellows. With such rich vital stuff we did not ask for plot.

After this Act the President of the Society came on and said that the Society was now dead, but all contributions would be gratefully received.

And in the last Act, when the eagerly awaited climax came, and *Pearl*, the Pig-woman, fell flat on her face with a pan of hot grease, the enthusiasm knew no bounds; all those pale and wearied people became suddenly alive, stirred to their depths by the wholesome spirit of the seventeenth century. One thought with shame of the vulgar knockabout buffoonery of such productions as *What's Yours?*

"Jolly good show," said George, with approval. "Sort of *revue*, really – wasn't it?"

"*George!*" I said. "What *do* you mean?"

---

1. "If you've never been vamped by a brown girl
   You've never been vamped at all."

THE ANNUAL DINNER

Clubs are of two kinds – (1) the ordinary Social Club, which is designed to discourage human intercourse and as far as possible exempt a man from the use of speech; and (2) the Dining Club, which deliberately encourages both. At the former, one is conscious always of the intense loathing men have for each other. But a Dining Club is obviously quite different.

Of this latter class perhaps the brightest is the Society of Beetles, to which George is this year secretary.

George has been a beetle for two or three years, and for two or three years I have successfully refused to attend a dinner of the Society as his guest. But when a man becomes secretary to anything, if it is only a Society of Beetles, you may as well do what he wants at once and avoid further trouble. I went to the Annual Dinner.

The Beetles dine at seven o'clock at the Café Splendide on the third Friday in the month, unless it is Good Friday, Christmas Day, or the Birthday of the Founder, when Rule 27 applies. The third Friday in the month appears to be a popular day for private dinners, and I found a crowd of men studying a list that hung in the hail of the *café*:

JAPANESE GOLFING SOCIETY	Blenheim Room
VERMIN REPRESSION LEAGUE	Versailles Room
OLD POMPEIANS FC	Morelli Room
BEETLES	Santiago Room

A waiter, with uncanny instinct, segregated the anti-rat experts from the Japanese golfers, and herded the Beetles towards the Santiago vestibule, from which a roar of happy conversation emerged – a very frightening sound.

A huge flunkey, with a suspicious eye, stooped from an immense height and growled, "What is your *name*, Sir?"

"Oh, don't bother," said I, terrified. "Just say 'Haddock' – or anything like that."

"MISTER HADDUK!" bawled the man, and fifty chattering Beetles stopped chattering together and fixed their terrible eyes upon me.

Mr Rogers, the Grand Beetle, stepped forward – a fine old man, with an ebony staff and wearing a magenta tie. On his breast, suspended by a chain of gold (or some similar metal), the Gold Beetle blazed.

"We are so pleased that you could come," said this terrific figure.

"So are we," I said stupidly, and we stared at each other in a friendly way, wondering what to say next.

For such moments I have only one remark which, as a rule, gloriously fills the breach.

"Let me see," I said respectfully. "Where did I meet you before, Sir?"

"We have never met before," said the Grand Beetle without hesitation

"No," I said, "we haven't," and kind of melted into the crowd.

George appeared, in a proper state of secretarial dither and importance and introduced me to Brother Beetle Scragg, a Past-Grand-Beetle, who wore a green tie and a green sash across his breast, and was nevertheless exceedingly morose.

"Yes, it's a jolly little club," said Brother Scragg "One keeps up with old friends – and so forth. 'Course, I don't come much myself," he added gloomily. "Haven't been here for *years*. Hullo, Streak! How are you? Don't often see *you* here."

"No," said little Mr Streak. "First time for three years. You're looking older"; and he passed on.

"Now *that*," said Mr Scragg confidentially, lowering his voice – "*that's* a man I can't stand, Not at any price. Don't you agree, Rowland?"

"Awful feller," said George heartily.

Just then an elderly man with fierce moustaches rushed up. "Look here, Rowland," he said, "what on earth d'you put me next to Crome for? If I'd known he was coming I'd never have – "

"Awfully sorry, Mr Jubb," said George; "I thought you were at school together."

"So *we were*," snapped Jubb.

At dinner I sat between George and Brother Streak, with Brother Scragg close by. Brother Streak was expansive.

"Ha!" he said, with a genial look round the room. "Ought to be a jolly evening. There's nothing like a Dining Club, I always say, for bringing men together. Here we are, doctors, lawyers, civil servants, all the professions, scattered about, and never run across each other in the ordinary way from one year's end to another. Get out of touch. Then we meet like this in a jolly friendly way, have a jolly evening – quaint old customs and all that; and we're all as jolly – as jolly – "

"As sandboys," I suggested.

"Exactly. Yes," he mused aloud, gulping an oyster, "any number of old friends I've got here. Now there's Rigby – that skinny little devil at the corner. He was at Balliol in my time. Clever fellow, very. Civil servant. But I don't see much of him nowadays. Something funny about him."

"He looks a little aloof," I ventured.

"*Aloof!*" said Mr Streak with sudden passion. "Aloof isn't the word. Stand-offish, I call it. *Conceited ass!* Just because he's – Why, do *you* know – ?"

Mr Streak paused, choking.

"Mr Scragg's a friend of yours, isn't he?" I put in hastily.

"Scragg? Ah, yes; I saw you talking to him. Look here," he whispered, "you're a young man and I'm an old one. Now you be careful of Scragg I've known him since he was a boy, and he's got a kind of cheery, hail-fellow-well-met manner with him that takes young men in – if they trust him. *Then he picks their brains!*"

"Good God!" I said, aghast, and looked furtively at the cheery brain-picker, who was then picking a pheasant-bone with extreme gloom.

"Yes," said Streak. "That's what he does. I don't often take a dislike to a man, but if I'd known those two fellows would be here I'd never have come, much as I enjoy it. O *Lord!*"

At this point the entire company rose, still chewing, while the Arch-Beetle solemnly handed to the Grand Beetle the Silver Bumble and the Wand of Office. The Grand Beetle made a short speech in Latin and we returned to our birds.

"Funny old custom," said George.

"Jolly," I said politely.

"Damn nonsense," said Streak, "giving everybody indigestion. Not a bad wine, this, is it?"

"I *say*, Streak," said Scragg in a loud whisper, leaning across, "why on *earth* did they make old Rogers 'Grand'? He's the worst chairman – "

"Can't think," said Streak happily. "Can't *imagine*. I never *saw* such a chairman. Never in all my life!"

"Just what *I* was saying," said Scragg; and it was pleasant to see the warm glance of sympathy which passed between the two old friends.

After the loyal toasts the Grand Beetle rose and said that "No speeches" was the rule of the Club.

He said that Brother Beetle Twiston was seriously ill in South America, and would be glad, he was sure, to know that they were thinking of him...

Scragg groaned.

"One word more." (When I hear those words I sit back in my chair and prepare for a good long speech.) Brother Beetles would be glad to know that the History of the Club was now ready, and a mere cheque for thirty shillings would secure a copy. Brother Beetle Carver's labours...

Streak groaned. "My hat! *That* feller!"

The speech continued.

One word more...

One word more and then he had done... (Scragg tore his hair.)

He did not wish to detain them, but there was just *one* thing. (Streak closed his eyes and snorted.)

And now he had finished...

But, before he sat down...

He knew quite well that nobody wished to listen to *him*, but he really could not sit down without...

When he did sit down, the toasts of "The Guests," "The Club," "The Army," "The Navy," "The Grand Beetle," "The Arch-Beetle" (the last drunk kneeling), were proposed at some length by various mature Beetles, each of whom made it quite clear that he was in no sense making a speech. The night wore on. The minutes of the last meeting were read and carried with considerable enthusiasm, and a new member, an elderly solicitor, was struck thrice in the face with the Wand of Office to confirm his Beetledom. Streak and Scragg made no attempt to conceal their hatred and contempt for the whole proceedings, and fell at last into a sort of stupor, broken only by occasional snorts and muttered execrations.

But at the end, about midnight, Streak said, "You ought to join us, my boy. Jolly little club – isn't it?"

"Thanks, I belong to one Dining Club already," I said. "Only it's rather different, of course. We're all the same age, you see, and we were all together at Oxford – all friends in a way. Quite simple, you know – no speeches or anything. Still, it's rather jolly."

"I know," said Streak, with a sudden far-off sadness in his eyes. "That's how *this* Club began."

FINANCE

This is the season of Company Meetings. At the first hint of Spring a certain liveliness seems to stir the Limited Liability world, and with one accord the Companies get together and have things out. No shareholder should miss these functions. You, Sir, who invariably fling your Notice Convening an Ordinary General Meeting into the waste-paper basket, with a harsh comment on the dividend; you, Madam, who do not even read the admirable report of the Chairman's admirable address in the Commercial Column – what are you? You are mere *rentiers*, and functionless *rentiers* at that. To furnish capital and draw dividends is not enough; unless you take a practical hand in the destinies of your Company you are betraying your trust, and risking your money. Who knows what these City sharks may not be up to? True, they send you elaborate balance-sheets, elaborately countersigned by Chartered Accountants. But if you examine these accounts you will find that they are just as fishy as your own, and full of the same old dodges. What are these shadowy "Sundries" and "General Charges" and "Sundry Creditors?" Why it takes me back to my schooldays; only then we called it SPG[1] and the item seldom ran to £50,000. No, Sir, you must keep an eye on your Company.

And I have long felt uneasy about my investments in the Baralong and Boona Railway, in which I hold ten shares, either Ordinary, Preference, or Cumulative Participating Preference, I never quite know which. Possibly Debentures. Though probably, if the truth were known, what I have is ten quite common Shares.

At any rate I am always invited to the meetings, and this year I went. I crept into the room a little nervously, expecting a great crowd, for I have always understood that any talk of political unrest and so forth is speedily re-echoed in financial circles. The room was small and full of fog, and in it there were two men. One of them was a fellow-shareholder, bubbling with a pleased excitement and cross-examining an official of the Company about the balance-sheet. My heart warmed to him. Here at least was a conscientious colleague. I sat down next to him and determined to give him all possible assistance.

"That's an Asset in Suspense," said the official – a shifty fellow, I thought.

"Ah," said the shareholder wisely, "I see."

Baffled, he developed a new attack, talking very rapidly and in muffled tones. The official listened with a foxy smile. Then he said, "No, Sir, that's *here*, you see," and, seizing the Balance-Sheet, he quickly turned the pages and pointed. I peeped over the shareholder's shoulder and read:

CONTINGENCIES ACCOUNT £50,000

"Ah," said the shareholder – "of course."

He was baffled again. I decided not to help him any more.

Three more men sidled in, and after them an elderly lady. Now there were six of us.

All about the room were large maps of India, and, peering at these through the fog, I caught at last the meaning of Empire. There went the Baralong and Boona Railway, for which I had assumed so grave a responsibility – there it went through Baralong and Pindi, down the Dug Valley, off to Faikoot, over a range of mountains and down through Kutlej to Chittagore, and so to Boona. All marked in red.

The fog thickened. No one spoke. We looked at each other with some suspicion. Another man came in and sat down hastily by the door, like men who come in to a wedding at the wrong time. Now there were seven of us.

The door of the Board Room opened and five old men tottered out and fell heavily into five chairs at the big table.

I dislike meetings at which there is no applause or other show of feeling, so at this event I clapped my hands together. No one joined me. The other six shareholders looked surprised, and just a little shocked; and over the rugged faces of the Directors there passed almost imperceptibly an expression of self-consciousness combined with gratification and a distaste for crude emotion. I realised that I had struck the wrong note, and I thought suddenly of one of the more sombre plays of M MAETERLINCK, in which six blind old men and six blind old women (one mad) are discovered sitting on dead leaves discussing a priest who turns out to be dead also. That was the note. Only I hoped the Railway was not dead.

The Oldest Old Man rose shakily and, clinging to the table, began to read from a long document. I listened eagerly. What teeming plans of expansion would the wise old Empire-builder reveal? What new developments? What Branch-lines? And what had he done with my ten pounds?

He read quaveringly, addressing his words to his beard, and not all of them reached me; but I heard him falter:

"*The permanent way of your railway is in excellent condition.*"

"*Your* railway!" I thrilled. All the seven shareholders – all the £2,500,000 Ordinary and Preference Capital Created and £1,500,000 Raised by Debenture Stock which we represented – all thrilled. Thank heaven at least the permanent way was well!

"*The Pilgrim traffic is satisfactory; the Rice traffic has been disappointing.*"

Ah, the brave pilgrims! I saw them, the dark-skinned, brown-eyed, holy men, huddled piously in their third-class carriages – or, rather, my third-class carriages – journeying on in the hard, dry light, from Baralong to Pindi, down the Dug Valley, on through Kutlej to Chittagore, and so to Boona, thinking perhaps of the bad old days when pilgrims had to walk to Boona. How they must thank me in their hearts for giving them a railway! Faithful fellows, they at least had kept the Old Line running!

And now the Second Oldest Old Man was speaking. He had recently visited India and seen *my* Railway. Real stations it has, and real engines – for he has seen them – and they are all "efficiently maintained." He too speaks kindly of the permanent way. The monsoon of 1922 was a good one. The rupee, however, is slack. But the pilgrims…! and he adds:

"*Attention is being paid to Arboriculture.*"

And this, for the benefit of his purely European audience, he translates: "Trees are being grown at the stations." Trees! These trees provide shade. In the shade of these trees – *my* trees – the pilgrims – *my* pilgrims – sit, thinking gratefully of the shareholders. I thrilled once more.

The Oldest Old Man sighed heavily and rose again. He spoke now in a kind of squeak, and an apologetic squeak at that, as if he feared the assembled multitude of shareholders would up and rend him.

He moved, in lengthy terms, that a dividend of ten per cent be paid to all of us. "I won't say I don't wish it was fifteen, as usual," he added less formally – the human little man. "Still, ten per cent is not to be sneezed at," he squeaked, and sank exhausted into his seat.

No one sneezed at him. No man blew his nose or protested in any way. "Carried!" he whispered. There was no applause. Our thoughts were far, far away.

Oh, Empire. Oh, the Monsoon! Oh, the Pilgrims!

The Oldest Old Man clutched at the table, sighed twice, and, abandoning the effort, said sitting:

"Will one of the Proprietors propose the re-election of the Auditors?"

And his eyes fell upon me.

No man calls me a Proprietor for nothing. What if the Balance-Sheet was bogus from cover to cover? What of "Sundries" and "Contingencies?" I was one of the Company. I too would strike a blow for Empire.

I rose and said, as eloquently as it is possible to say the words, "I move that Messrs. Budge, Foodie, and Runcorn be re-elected Auditors to our Railway."

Another Proprietor almost rose from his chair, and, moving his lips inaudibly, was understood to second the motion.

Silently the seven hands went up, heavy with destiny. "Carried," sighed the Chairman.

There was no applause.

So ended this Ordinary but Memorable General Meeting.

Oh, Empire! Oh, the Monsoon! Oh, Ten per cent!

---

1. Something – probably grub.

CHARITY

Far-off in Wapping, Joe Bundle stood moodily at the tiller of a coal-barge and, spitting into the Pool of London, emphatically reviled the order of society.

Ungrateful dog! For at that very moment some thirty of the best and noblest and richest in the land were labouring stealthily in Belgravia for the Wapping Mission to Bargees and Watermen.

But I anticipate. Life had been a whirl that week. Jaded with pleasure, I was seriously proposing to dine quietly in my own house when George rang up. "Come and sing," he said. "Belgravia Glee-Singers. Five o'clock."

"What for?"

"Charity. I dunno. Barges or something. Jolly good thing."

"Where do we sing?"

"In the streets. Come at five. Half an hour's practice first."

I felt that a little chastening, unselfish work for others would be good for me. I went.

The Belgravia Glee-Singers gathered unobtrusively in a drawing-room a quarter of a mile long. The proportions of the choir were startling. There seemed to be two Basses, one Tenor, twelve Altos, and seventeen Sopranos. At the first, and only, practice it appeared that George had been the only Bass, and the Basses had been voted a little weak. However, the choir was now complete. "Do good by stealth" is its motto, and everyone was provided with a mask to avoid attracting attention and prevent recognitions, also a dainty little electric torch; while many carried actual copies of the songs which it was proposed to perform.

Tea was served.

Lady Taffeta Blood was the best-dressed Soprano there. "Let's go," she said at last, eager for the good work.

"Oh, but we must put on our *masks*!" said Lady Miranda Tulle, who was easily the best-dressed Alto.

People who write books and ballets about masks imagine that these disguises are clapped on and off by ladies in the twinkling of an eye. In real life this is not so. The Sopranos and Altos trooped out of the room to adjust their masks. The Tenors and Basses adjusted their masks where they were, and sat down quietly for a long time.

Champagne was served.

When the ladies at length returned a striking transformation was seen. It is astonishing how much difference a tiny mask will make. Lady Taffeta Blood was, if anything, better dressed than before. She wore a simple but provocative mask of black satin, a provoking Spanish comb seven inches high, a challenging veil of black lace which entirely covered her forehead, a defiant dress of black velvet, and a maddening black cloak. She was more devastating than ever. The disguise was complete.

The other ladies were similarly disguised. Some of them inquired with apprehension if they were likely to be recognised, but it was clear that they had no real fear.

"Hadn't we better practise a little?" said someone.

"No time now," said everyone sadly.

"My mask tickles," said Lady Blain.

We trooped out into the cold wet night.

"Jolly plucky of all these women to go tramping round the streets for the poor," said George.

"Isn't it?" I said.

We entered seven high-powered motorcars and were rapidly driven to Lady Lowbrow's. Here our hardships began. Huddled in the vast cold hall we sang, "Blow away the Morning Dew," in four parts and three keys. Four parts? Nay, there were more than that. The six principal Sopranos had powerful and beautiful voices, and these, led by Lady Taffeta, burst into song immediately they entered the house. The other Sopranos, crowding in after them, began unfortunately a bar behind, but by the end of the first verse had all but caught them up. A similar competition was to be observed among the Altos, where none sang faster than Lady Blain. The Tenor, unhappily, was never able to enter the house at all for the crowd of Press-men and photographers. As for the Basses, George and I were penned in a dark corner behind a Greek statue, where it was impossible to see music or expand lungs. But we did what we could.

George sang:

"Upon the sweetest summer-time,
Ah-wa-wa-wa-wa-wa,
Ah-la-la-la! my eyelashes
Keep catching in my mask –
    And sing, BLOW away the morning dew!
Ah-wa! Wa-wa-wa!
Haven't you got an electric torch?
Ah, wa-wa-wa-la-*la!*"

I sang (but more beautifully):

"Upon the sweetest – la-la-la!
This *is* a jolly house.
A something, something I espied –
I wish I knew the words.
    And sing, BLOW away the morning dew!
I know, so do mine –
La-la-la-la-la-la-la-la –
The blasted thing is broke!"

It had been agreed that we should sing four verses only, but it had never been finally decided which. The Altos therefore finished off with the seventh verse, and the bulk of the Sopranos with the fourth, while the Basses carried on as before. All Lady Lowbrow's footmen, butlers, and domestic staff were clustered at the other end of the hall, and I looked at them with some nervousness. Surely we should now be forcibly ejected!

The footmen clapped with dignity. Lady Lowbrow came forth and presented us with a cheque for twenty pounds.

"Charity covers a multitude of sings," said Lady Taffeta daringly.

Two Press-men then took flashlight photographs of the assembled choir. To avoid publicity we retained our masks; and but for the list of names which was printed under the picture in the illustrated papers the identities of the singers would have remained an absolute mystery.

Champagne was served.

Tired but dauntless we resumed the quest. Outside it was raining hard, but we did not hesitate to enter the waiting cars and drive off to Lady Highbrow's. There are those who complain that it is difficult to extract money from the rich. This is base. All that is needed is to approach them *in the right way*.

And one such way is Music.

Lady Highbrow's butler met us at the door with a cheque for twenty-five pounds.

"How *sweet!*" said Lady Crêpe de Chine. "But doesn't she want us to *sing?*"

"No, milady," said the man, and shut the door.

Forty-five pounds already! The gay girls danced for joy. Wapping was in all our minds. The future of Wapping was already golden.

"Where shall we go now?" cried Lady Miranda. "Who's *really* rich?"

"I know one," said a slim girl, whose simple furs and old-fashioned pearl necklace scarcely suggested a large acquaintance with the wealthy. "Let's go to Berkeley Street."

We drove to Berkeley Street. The rain had stopped, and there in the open street, on the damp pavement, the ladies sang "The Lass of Richmond Hill." The Basses, by a misunderstanding, sang "Oh, don't deceive Me!" but were not detected. A crowd gathered. The sweet old folk-music of the people charmed all hearts. Lord Shake sent out his little girl with a cheque for forty pounds. For this princely contribution we offered to sing again. "Name your song!" we cried. "No, no, you mustn't waste your time on me," said the courtly man. "Go on with the good work – go and sing to somebody else."

We walked on to Lady Canute's, and sang "The Wraggle-Taggle Gipsies" in the porch. She flung us a cheque from the drawing-room. Her husband flung us five-pound notes from the billiard-room. Her daughters tore off their jewels and rings and cast them out of an upper window. Lady Taffeta gathered the lot.

We shouted our gratitude; they waved it aside. But we insisted on entering the house to render our thanks with due ceremony.

Cocktails and sandwiches were served.

And now we were keyed up to any sacrifice. Another effort or two, and Wapping should never know want again. We attacked the hotels.

First snatching a hasty snack – nothing more than oysters, soup entrée, sweet, and savoury, washed down with a light champagne – we rose up in the great Blue Room of the "Fitz" and sang "Drink to me only with thine Eyes." Then we sang "Mowing the Barley," "Hares on the Mountains," "Creeping Jane," and "The Merry Haymakers." The diners loved it. They sat spellbound, drinking only with their eyes and not asking for wine, partly because the choir cut off half the room from all communication with the waiters. For five minutes no food or drink came near those particular tables. Then a man more sensitive than the others stood up and offered us five pounds. The others quickly followed his example. Lady Taffeta took round the hat. It overflowed.

Only one slight cloud darkened our joy. It was here that Lady Taffeta was recognised. A man had seen through her disguise.

"The *shame* of it!" the poor girl whimpered.

Two hundred pounds in one evening – by the mere power of Song! Song and Unselfishness!

Yet far off in Wapping Joe Bundle stood moodily at the tiller of a barge and, spitting into the Pool of London, reviled emphatically the order of society.

The dog!

CLUB LIFE; OR, GETTING AN APPETITE

For an old club-man I go but seldom to my club. An occasional hasty lunch, a cup of coffee in the billiard-room, and a generous donation to the Servant's Christmas-box – that is my club-life. I have never read a book in the Library, never played billiards in the Billiard-room, or fives in the Fives-court. It would be far cheaper to resign and take the lunches at the Ritz.

But I constantly drive past the place on an omnibus and observe its windows with pride and wonder. I have even had to sit silent while other passengers exercised their cheap and offensive wit on the row of hairless heads hung out like lanterns along the smoking-room window. And on each occasion I realise anew how little I know of my club. Whose are those heads, for example? And are the heads I see at half-past two the same as the heads I see when I drive homeward again at half-past six? And, if so, have they been there ever since?

To answer these and other questions I determined, the other day, to be a club-man in good earnest! and naturally I took as my model old Shrike.

Old Shrike has pink cheeks and white whiskers, and he walked up the steps before me about 1.15. Once within the door a sigh of satisfaction escaped him as the monastic and congenial atmosphere wrapped him about. He nodded fiercely, and without speaking, to the hall-porter, and swept into the wash-room, where he encountered Potts, a favourite crony, plump but gloomy.

"Mornin'," said Shrike, and "Mornin'," growled Potts.

While they washed the conversation continued.

For twenty-five years there has been a pipe which rattles when the tap is turned on – an unfailing barometer by which to judge the pressure of life upon the nerves and spirits of the members.

"Why don't they do something to this *tap*?" said Potts querulously.

"What's the matter with it?" said Shrike, and went upstairs.

In the dining-room he selected a seat at the unpopulated end of the long table, propped up *The Weekly Patriot* against a water-jug, and remarked to the Waiter, "Club Lunch – Thick – Small Bass." After that he did not speak again.

By about half-past two the big smoking-room was nearly empty. Twenty minutes later there were only four of us in the windows. Outside the sun shone merrily, but for some reason we kept our backs to the light.

The fourth man sighed, finished his coffee, drained his liqueur-brandy glass for the last time, sighed, rose, and shuffled out.

Shrike cleared his throat, as one who can now speak freely.

"How've you been keeping?" he said.

"I'm not at all well," said Potts.

"Liver?"

"Appetite – can't eat my breakfast."

"I eat a good breakfast. But I can't get my dinner down."

"I eat a good dinner. You don't take enough exercise."

"I have to be careful. My heart troubles me."

"Thought you'd got over that."

"Got over it? Huh! I've been very seedy lately. Very seedy. Very seedy indeed."

"You're not looking the same."

There was a long silence.

Potts regretfully discarded the last three centimetres of his cigar.

"What are you doing this afternoon?" he asked.

"I shall take a turn in the Park presently," said Shrike.

"I'll join you," said Potts. "Get an appetite."

Then there was a very long silence.

Then there was a long low rumble.

Then there was another rumble.

I opened *The Man With Three Ears*.

"I shall take a turn afterwards," said Potts at teatime. "Just a constitutional."

"The food's very bad here," said Shrike, taking a second slice of muffin. "They can't toast a muffin nowadays. Don't know how it is."

"Don't know how you can *eat* those things. If I had one of them I'd never be able to look my doctor in the face again," said Potts, helping himself to buttered toast.

"Quite wholesome, if they're well done," said Shrike. "I'm not feeling the thing today."

"You ought to play golf."

"Couldn't do it. Heart wouldn't stand it."

"You coddle yourself."

"Have to."

"I'll take you for a brisk walk afterwards. Fresh air's what you want."

"I must write a few letters first," said Shrike, closing his eyes.

A little later George came in with two other young men.

"Thought I'd look in and read the papers," he said, and he picked up a heavy portfolio labelled TITTLE-TATTLE – RAKES' CLUB – NOT TO BE TAKEN AWAY.

I returned to the engrossing mystery of *The Man With Three Ears*. The two young men talked golf-shop in a hushed whisper. Potts watched George reading. And well he might.

George sat back comfortably and prepared for reading. He drew from his pocket a substantial cigarette-case and carefully selected a cigarette. He pinched it, shook it, and tapped it delicately on a table. Then he laid it down and slowly produced an amber cigarette-holder. He smoothed back his hair, inserted the cigarette in the holder, and finally lit it.

Then he opened the portfolio and revealed a long piece of elastic.

"Damn," said George.

Shrike opened his eyes – more in anger than in sorrow.

George fetched *Gossip* and began again. He is a patient, steady reader and misses nothing; and, generous soul, he likes to share his pleasure with others.

"Look at this," he said, very soon.

"This" was a page which proved conclusively, as well by pictorial evidence as by the printed word, that various ladies and gentlemen of distinction had been present at a race-meeting the previous week.

"That's Joan Thistle," said George.

The picture in question appeared to my jaundiced eyes to represent the back view of three women standing under umbrellas, two elderly and one young (judging by proportions).

"Oh!" I said, tearing myself away from Sâsh, the woman with the Tiger's Eyes. "Friend of yours?"

"No," said George; "but she's engaged to a man I know."

"By Jove!" I said, and returned to Tiger-Eye.

A few minutes later he said, "There she is again."

"Who?" I asked angrily.

"Joan," said George.

I looked and found that George was still at the same page. This time Joan Thistle was standing with an elderly man who carried field glasses. One had a side view of Joan's figure, and if her head had not been turned away one would have been able to see her profile.

"Jolly pretty girl," said George.

"Pity they didn't photograph her face."

"Yes; it's not very good of her," said George solemnly, and stared at the picture again, as if he could scarcely believe the evidence of his eyes. But there it was, in the plainest of print:

A FLUTTER AT WHITWICK. LADY JOAN THISTLE CHATS WITH A FRIEND

George took a last look at Joan, slowly turned the page and gazed profoundly at Constance Claire Among her Pets. Shrike closed his eyes again. I returned to Sâsh and read through the discovery of the dead wolf-hound, the night in the tomb, and the second appearance of the Bloody Arrow.

Then George plucked my sleeve. "See this?" he whispered. "Constance Claire."

"Friend of yours?"

"No; Tommy knows her."

"Oh!"

Thus the evening wore on in perfect placidity. George waded methodically through *Gossip*, finding on every page pictures of people who were personally acquainted with people he himself knew, and ending gloriously with the Motoring Section, where Joan was to be seen driving a Bonbon. Meanwhile the eyes of Sâsh grew more disturbing every moment, Shrike snored more shamelessly, and the two young men gradually approached the eighteenth hole.

But about six a certain uneasiness pervaded the quiet room. Shrike woke up with what is known as a start and gazed stupidly at the clock. The young men were suddenly silent, and fidgeted.

"What about our constitutional?" said Potts.

Shrike made no reply.

"Well, I shall take a turn," said Potts, rising laboriously. "Get an appetite for dinner. Coming?"

Shrike said nothing, continuing to gaze at the clock. But a sort of radiance spread over his face, as if he had at last discovered what time it was.

At the word "appetite" George too looked sharply at the clock; and he deposited Gossip on the floor.

"*What about an appetizer?*" he whispered.

One of the young men hitched his eyebrows at his companion, who shrugged his shoulders in return.

George rang the bell.

Mr Potts sat down again.

THE PHARISEES[1]

"At Stamford Bridge," I read, "the Pensioners will entertain the Saints, when some bright football is expected."

"What's that?" said George.

"Chelsea play Southampton. Second round of the Cup. Let's go."

"Professional football? Not much!" said George. "It's a filthy game."

"Did you ever see one?"

"No. But I don't approve of it. And I don't approve of all those thousands of people just *watching* a game on Saturdays. They ought to be playing themselves. Let's go and see the Harlequins."

"We'll go and see Chelsea," I said firmly. "You live in Cheyne Walk, and you ought to support them. You'll see lots of people you know."

"Shall I?"

"Of course. All Tite Street will be there."

"Oh, well!" said George.

With sixty-seven thousand other members of the proletariat we fought our way through the turnstiles, George in a state of increasing rebellion and distaste. He is a bad man to take about among the proletariat, and there was an "incident" almost immediately.

" 'Oo are you shoving?" said a rat-like little man with extreme truculence as we emerged upon the ground.

"*You!*" said George brutally and shoved again.

"I'd push yer face in, if it wasn't a Cup tie," said the man, and scampered off into the crowd.

George in his immaculate bowler suggests extreme wealth, and as one man the Chelsea hawkers made for him.

"Oo'll 'ave a blood-orange?" said one. " 'Ere y'are, Sir. Two bloods a penny!" But George would not have a blood-orange.

" 'Ere y'are, *The Daily Liar!*" another was shouting. "Over a thousand laughs for one penny. Yer can't stop laughin'. 'Ere y'are, Sir. Over a thousand laughs for one penny. Over a thousand laughs for tuppence," he corrected as he saw George.

George refused this tempting offer also. Nor would he buy a rattle, a penny balloon, or a celluloid baby in the colours of the Saints.

"I don't see anybody I know," he said plaintively.

We climbed a mountainous bank and stood behind and a little below the last row of the sixty-seven thousand. From here one had a superb view of their hats and the backs of their necks. One judged by the cheering and the conversation that a football match was being played somewhere in the neighbourhood.

Two young men stood placidly beside us – short men who could see even less than we could. They had, however, a friend in the back who *could* see something, and through his eyes they enjoyed the game.

" 'Ow much can yer see now, Bert?" said one.

"I can see 'arf the grahnd nah," said Bert.

" 'Ow's the gime?" said Bill.

"Jimmy's got the ball nah. – Come *ahn*, Jimmy!"

"Wot's 'e doin' with it?" said Tom, sucking an orange.

" 'E's kicked it aht."

"Sit dahn in front!" shouted Bert, dancing excitedly. "Nah Barrer's got it. Come ahn, Barrer! Come *ahn!*" Then came a terrible snarl of disappointment. "*Aow!*"

"Wot's 'e done?" said Bill.

" 'E kicked it aht."

The Man About Town

"Go on?" said Bill, and he drew a bottle of beer from his pocket.

"Taime, ain't it?" said Bill, after a pause.

"You're right," said Tom, gazing at the Underground Railway. "Ow's Tyler shapin'?"

"Rotten. 'E's got the ball nah. Come ahn, Tyler! Come ahn, lad! *Aow!*"

"Wot's 'appened, Bert? Don't keep it all to yerself."

" 'E kicked it be'ind. Right in front of goal – the – chump!"

"Go on?" said Tom. "Let's 'ave a suck at that, Bill."

"Aw-right, mate. Don't waste none of it."

Bill had a go at the orange and Tom had a go at the bottle.

"Taime, ain't it?" said Bill.

"You're right," said Tom. "Ain't been a fahl yet – 'as there, Bert?"

"The Saints was 'eld up for 'andlin' – that's all."

"Go on?"

I love the incredulity with which Bill receives the simplest statements of fact. This is a conversational device common to all classes: only in the best circles we say "Really?"

We watched the game in this way for some twenty minutes. By that time both the bottle and the orange were dry, and the spirit of adventure had entered into Tom and Bill.

"Come ahn," said Bill; "I've 'ad enough er this."

"Over the top, boys!" cried Tom; and, lowering their heads, they butted into the vast crowd. George and I shoved too, but, of course, in a more gentlemanly way. Cries of protest were raised.

"Can't help it, mates," lied Tom. "They're shovin' be'ind. Gawd, Bill, I can see a bit of the grass!"

"You're lucky. I can't see nothink only Bert."

"Mike room in front, please," called Tom, like a constable. " 'Ere's a poor lady can't see nothink."

The chivalrous crowd parted, and we suddenly found ourselves with a magnificent view of the sixty-seven thousand, not to speak of the twenty-two.

The twenty-two were running actively from place to place, heading the ball cunningly, feinting cleverly, sometimes pretending they were about to kick the ball forward and then kicking it behind them with their heels, sometimes not kicking at all; in fact they displayed every trick of the footballer's art except that of actually kicking the ball through the goal.

"Taime, ain't it?" said Tom, after a little of this.

"You're right," said Bill.

Most of the crowd seemed to agree, except those who had brought rattles and rattled them impartially whenever the ball went out. The others cheered occasionally, but without spirit. "And they call this football!" George groaned.

But at last one of the Saints' forwards got the ball on the wing. An inoffensive little man, he prepared to kick it into the centre, meaning no harm. And one of the Pensioners' defenders, the valiant Tyler, a huge man with a torso like a prize-fighter, flung himself five feet through the air, met the little man somewhere about the point of the chin, and bore him crumpled to the ground.

"*Fahl!*" yelled the Saints' supporters, and booed with a will.

"Yus, that was a proper fahl," said Tom judicially.

"Can't expect nothink else in a Cup tie," said Bert.

The little man still rolled prostrate on the ground, and still the outraged Saints called Heaven to witness the crime.

This at last annoyed Bill. " 'Old yer rah!" he shouted. "What's the matter with yer?"

"Wot abaht that dirty fahl?" said one of the Saints.

"Wasn't a dirty fahl?" cried Tom.

"I tell you it *was* a dirty fahl. See?"

"Where's yer manners?" said Bill.

"Good old Tyler!" shouted Bert, and so said many of the loyal Pensioners about him.

The game was renewed, but now everyone enjoyed it, including George. No goals were scored, it is true, but fouls, off-sides, and free kicks were scored in quick succession, and there was never a dull moment. The Saints sinned frequently, and every time we went into an ecstasy of self-righteous horror.

"Fairplay, now!" Bill shouted warningly.

"Dirty dogs!" said Bert, with great enjoyment.

Whenever the ball accidentally touched the hands of a player we shouted " '*Ands!*" as if the man had poisoned a baby; and whenever a Chelsea man fell to the ground we shouted "*Fahl!*" in case he had been tripped and the referee had missed it.

"This is great," said George.

And if we enjoyed seeing a good foul, how much more did the players enjoy it? As one man they stopped in their tracks and raised appealing hands to Heaven, their faces masks of outraged virtue. Sometimes a player was hurt; and how *he* enjoyed it! How he hung upon his fellows' necks, writhing and grimacing, groaning and closing his eyes, and scarce daring to put the injured foot to the ground. And when he did, what a rousing cheer we gave the hero as he bounded away like a rabbit to his place!

No goals were scored; but, after all, four thousand pounds were taken at the gate, and sixty-seven thousand people thoroughly enjoyed themselves.

Bill summed up the game. "I reckon the Saints did more dirty work than wot we did."

"You're right," said Bert.

"Good fun," said George. "But what an infernally filthy game!" he added hastily. "These fellows ought to go to a public school."

"They ought."

The following day I attended a great Labour Demonstration in Trafalgar Square, at which several speakers gave instructions to the Government.

"The old parties," said one of them, "are corrupt and dishonest. They have fooled you and cheated you and left you in a mess. And the Labour Party alone can get you out of it, because the Labour Party alone has clean hands."

"That's right!" said an enthusiastic voice.

And there was dear old Bert.

1. The original appearance of this trifle caused a little sensation in political circles, if I may judge from the flood of reproachful letters which I received from supporters of the Labour Party, assuring me that they had always loved my amusing articles about rich men in clubs, Mr Asquith, the National Party, and so on – but really, when it came to laughing at the Labour Party, there *were* limits… One gentleman kindly sent me a copy with certain passages generously underlined in red ink, and suggested with some warmth that "George" also ought to be included among the "Pharisees." Curiously enough, this had occurred to me; but I had no red ink; and without red ink it is so difficult to make one's points.

Other complained of my use of the word proletariat, the suggestion being, I gather, that that is not a word which ought to be used of a fellow-countryman who fought in the war. I agree.

SECRET GOLFING

At three a'clock on a dull December afternoon two young men might have been observed walking at a brisk pace along the odious thoroughfare of High Street, Kensington

Indeed, they *were* observed.

George Rowland was carrying a bag of golf clubs, shining, weighty, and formidable. The bag had an impressive waterproof lid to it, but this was thrown back so that the full splendour and variety of the clubs might be revealed. From the waist of the bag depended a ballsponge of costly and unusual design, and fixed to it was a tripod device by which the bag could be made to stand on its end at need, and thus relieve its owner of the intolerable strain of stooping to pick it up.

George himself was dressed in a provocative cloth cap, a tweed golfing-coat and breeches, stockings of the most fluffy wool, and heavy brogue shoes with soles of double thickness richly studded with clusters of three-inch nails.

The ends of his coloured garters dangled tastefully down the calves of his legs, and over his shoelaces there flapped contemptuously as he walked two substantial leather aprons, fringed with a valance of tiny leather tongues, and serving what purpose I have never been able to discover.

George strode arrogantly through the herd of shoppers, making no secret of the fact that he was dressed for golf on a week-day; and not a few of those whom he prodded inadvertently in the back with his driver or struck about the knees with the lower end of his bag turned to look with interest at the fresh-faced young athlete.

I too carried, but naked, a brassie and an iron; and I followed guiltily in George's wake, striving, however, to look like a man who has been buying brassies and irons for Christmas presents. I was dressed very simply. But for the shameless youth in front of me none would have guessed that I was about to play golf.

Or rather practise golf. For we were bound for the premises of the enterprising Day-and-Night Golf Club in Kensington. "It's nearly as good as the real thing," said George with enthusiasm. "Opens your shoulders, pulls your game together. You get the air, you get the exercise – "

"And you can wear the clothes."

"Well, I *can't* play golf in trousers," said George good-humouredly.

We bought two tickets, entitling us to half an hour's practice each. A small but uniformed caddie with a MARCEL grin ushered me into a kind of cubicle, curtained on three sides; and there I nervously removed my overcoat, with something of the sensation of persons about to confront a Medical Board.

The fourth side of the cubicle was open to the air, and about fifty yards away was a huge net, the size of a large house, and lettered at various heights A, B, C, and D. All the cubicles faced this common obstacle, and in front of each was a small but objectionable bunker.

Through the curtains on my left came the sound of a rhythmic panting and groaning, and at brief but regular intervals a golf-ball emerged into the open and entered one of the bunkers. In the west the Kensington sun was sinking.

The boy brought me a heap of sand. Then he brought me a basket containing ninety-six golf balls. Then he teed up one ball and stood expectant, grinning.

" 'It the A, Sir," he said. I swung my brassie...

He teed up the ball again, grinning.

"Do I use *all* these balls?" I said.

"Yes, Sir," he said. "Eight dozen on 'em."

I swung again. The ball struck the C belonging to the second cubicle to the right.

Now there were only ninety-five.

A little strenuous working and there were only eighty-nine. At this point Marcel departed quietly from the cubicle, grinning.

To be left alone with eighty-nine golf-balls is a great temptation. I sat down and lit a pipe.

The Kensington sun had set. The great net hung dimly in the dusk; beyond it the high trees grew dark and ghostly. I smoked contentedly.

It occurred to me that secret golfing is a very ugly thing.

Next door the sounds of laboured breathing and rhythmic physical exertion continued; and, occasionally, the sound of wood striking a hard ball. One man at least was seeing the thing through. On the other side George, too, was aiming balls in quick succession at the net, and as often as not hitting it.

"How goes it?" he cried cheerily. "Quite like the real thing, isn't it?"

"Quite," I said. "There's a terribly slow couple in front of me. I can't get on at all."

"Forty-five," counted George with satisfaction, and hit it clean over the net into the trees.

Forty-five. And I was eighty-nine, and sixteen minutes had gone. And I was wasting good money...

That wretched basket destroyed my peace. It fascinated me. I drew it towards me. Those reproachful balls – eighty-nine balls – two balls a penny – one must do *something* with them. I took one out. My fingers itched. I took out three...

For five minutes I was perfectly happy.

To juggle capably with three balls has long been one of my minor ambitions. Alas, in real life the opportunities for practising this art are sadly limited. Someone always wants to play tennis with the tennis-balls. Someone always wants to keep the oranges for eating. Here at last I had found the perfect place for juggling. Absolute privacy – unlimited material… I had long been no mean performer with two. In five minutes I was practically a master of three.

Then George peeped round the corner and caught me.

"What *are* you doing?" he gasped.

"Playing catch," I said. "It's really too dark for golf, isn't it?"

"Oh, but I'll soon put that right," he said confidently, and disappeared.

Sure enough almost immediately the cubicle was generously illuminated and a powerful searchlight was flung upon the net.

"*There!*" said George with pride, and resumed his game.

"I appeal against the light," I protested feebly, knowing well that there was now no hope. Somehow or other I must drive my eighty-nine balls into or towards the net, or I should stand condemned as a slacker – or, worse, a wastrel.

I took my brassie; I built fifteen tees in quick succession, and smote fifteen balls with vigour into the night.

Building tees in quick succession is exhausting work. I took my iron.

I leaned upon my iron and, breathless, mused a while.

The moon had risen. A sort of frenzy seemed to have possessed the golfers. On every side, with new devotion and with audible comments on Fate and kindred subjects, they smote their ninety-six balls into the weird unnatural light, seldom pausing to observe in which direction (if any) they went. And I thought, How great a thing is Civilisation and how noble a thing is Progress, in that our forefathers were content to play at the barbarous game of bowls in the broad noonday, while we in our wisdom can bang a golf-ball at the moon by the aid of electric light!

But I had five minutes to go. And seventy-four balls. How could I face Marcel again? Not to speak of George?

I too must render my tribute to Civilisation and the Spirit of Golf.

Stealthily I took a handful and flung them reverently at the moon, the queen of madness.

The subsequent handfuls, with no little skill, I rolled or tossed into the bunker on my left.

When George came in the basket was nearly empty. "Got any over?" he asked.

"Only three," I said.

BOHEMIA

George Rowland and I, incorrigible butterflies that we are, have yet our serious moments. We weary suddenly of rich hotels and rich food and the artificial gaiety of millionaires, and we long for some sweeter, simpler grade of life, where men and women who have not lost touch with primitive things genuinely enjoy themselves.

In such a mood George took me to the Café Splendide. "Great place for artists," he said. "Regular Bohemians, you know. See every sort of artist there – painters and – artists and – and painters – and so on. I saw Frome there once," he added modestly.

"Did you?" I said; for Frome in those days was a name to conjure with in artistic circles; I speak of several weeks ago.

"Does you good," said George, "to see a diff'rent kind of feller now and then – artists and painters – and poets, and so forth. Keeps you in touch."

"Right," I said, "Let's go."

George made it pretty plain that in Bohemia they were poor men and concentrated on realities, so we were careful not to overdress. George wore an ordinary black dinner-jacket, and a frilled soft shirt, with a sober black tie. I discarded my opera-hat for the occasion and wore an unobtrusive stetson of grey velours.

We had a cocktail at Boom's, a gin-and-bitters at the "Hell and Tommy," and strolled round to Spider's for an appetizer.

Then we dined quite simply at the Berkeley and took a taxi to the Café about ten.

The place fascinated me at once. I am one of those unfortunate people who always arrive everywhere at the wrong time. If I go to the House of Commons there is an unusually dull debate; if I go to the theatre the leading lady is ill; if I go away to the country the primroses are just over, the bluebells are not out, and the weather has just broken. I dare not go to the Zoo for fear the elephants will die.

But here I saw that for once fortune was with me. The Café was full of chattering, gay Bohemian people – simple unaffected creatures, exchanging busily, after a day's work in studio or study, the latest gossip of their craft. Their clothes, their faces, betrayed their character; and, had they not, the Café, exhaled a sufficiently revealing atmosphere of its own.

On one of the walls I saw in large letters the word

PILSEN.

On another

BIERE.

Somehow these homely legends sent a thrill through me. Here was real life at last. And then – the whole *ensemble!* One felt that all true followers of Art and Beauty must inevitably be drawn to this lively centre – to the cheap and misty looking-glasses which covered every wall, the hideous *caryatides* in coffee-coloured plaster, the unlovely marble tables, and the tawdry sofas of red plush.

We sat down and I ordered two beers. "*Si,*" said the waiter in Italian, and disappeared.

Then we surveyed the gay scene. Some way off, dimly discernible through the smoke, a large party of young men were making merry, and every now and then they rose and sang some jolly tipsy chorus in a foreign language.

"Art students," said George. "French, I fancy."

A harassed waiter flashed across the foreground. "One *bière*, one Pilsen," said George, who knew the ways of the place.

"*Si*," said the waiter in Spanish, and disappeared.

But all was not gay. Next to me sat a man in a black slouch hat, snuffing rhythmically and gazing with dejection at a glass of some pale-green liquid before him. One scented tragedy.

George nudged me. "Always here," he whispered. "Drinking himself to death. *Absinthe*."

"Good heavens!" I said. "Artist, I suppose?"

George nodded meaningly. Art – Ambition – Failure – Degradation – a whole life was in that nod.

While we spoke a waiter brought the man yet another of the wicked-looking glasses.

We ordered two absinthes.

I looked round me, trying to extract from the multitude of hoarse voices, pale cheeks, and weary eyes the secret, the essential spirit of the place. Was this little man the key – Disillusion – Decay?

It baffled me.

"Which is Frome?" I asked.

"Frome's not here tonight," said George apologetically. "And Daub's not here. And I don't see John Easel. Trigg's here very often – so is Waddle – but they're not here tonight. There's Badger, though – "

"What – the sculptor?"

"Yes, the sculptor. No, it isn't Badger. It's somebody else. Stark's not here either. In fact, it's rather a dull night. Pity. Most nights you see all sorts of int'r'sting people – artists – and painters and – and so forth."

"Never mind," I said. And indeed the strange exotic life I saw about me had an interest sufficient in itself without the false glamour of great names.

The Art students across the room sprang to their feet and drank a noisy toast, clinking their glasses and shouting excitedly. Two men with keen and lively faces sat down opposite to us and talked earnestly in low tones. Here and there one caught an Italian word.

And still beneath the gaiety and laughter, the clink of glasses, and the eager talk one seemed to hear that undertone of tragedy. Everywhere, I saw now, scattered among the chattering throng, there were lonely figures like the man beside me, with weary eyes and haggard faces, and those wicked little glasses before them...

This sense of misfortune oppressed me, and I strolled over and sat down near the Art students, who were singing the "Marseillaise." They at least were happy.

One of them rose as I arrived and made a little speech. He said: "Well, boys, we've 'ad a 'ard tussle of it, an' no mistake, but we've put two fences be'ind us, an' I say there's nothin' to prevent us goin' the 'ole way! 'Ere's to the old Rovers!"

They leapt to their feet and drank the toast with a Continental fire quite foreign to the phlegmatic Englishman.

"Who are they?" I asked a foreign-looking waiter, who looked his contempt at the question.

"Regent Rovers," he said. "Got through second round of the Cup today."

I stole back to George, and had to push past the two animated Italians

"*Guano!*" one of them was saying, with a terrible fury in his eyes. "*Guano!* Why, there's not another guano on the market to touch it! I *tell – you* – Steve, that ton for ton – "

The waiter had brought our absinthes, and I looked with some misgiving at the sinister drink.

A lump of sugar was poised upon a fretted spoon above each glass, and George was reverently dissolving the lumps with water. This, then, was the poison which had ruined so many lives – was even now ruining the life beside me...

I turned impulsively to the little man. Now he held a handkerchief to his eyes, and when he turned his face I saw that they were wet.

"Tell me," I said gently, "what is your trouble? I have many friends who are interested in Art, and if I can help you in any way – ?"

"Help?" he answered miserably. "If you can tell me who'll win the Three-o'clock tomorrow you can help. As for trouble, I've backed seven losers since Monday, and, if that isn't enough – " His voice trailed sadly into nothing, and I sipped my absinthe in confusion.

One sip was enough. I thrust the hateful stuff away. "George," I cried, "*it's cough mixture!*"

"It *is* rather like it," he admitted.

"That's right," said the little man. "Finest thing in the world for a cold. Always take it myself."

I looked again at the lonely tragic figures, with their weary eyes and wicked little glasses. And suddenly I knew their secret.

TATTERSALL'S

Life is full of strange adventures; but until I dropped into TATTERSALL'S with George Rowland I did not guess just how exciting it can be.

This Mr TATTERSALL lives at Knightsbridge, where every Monday he sells horses by auction; and you can tell the place by the number of rich motor-cars outside. One steps out of the jaded throng of shoppers into the vigorous air of the hunting field. The fascinating smell of the stable; the bronzed and dapper lieutenant-colonels; the dashing and oh, so faintly masculine ladies on the floor of the hail; the row of well-dressed charmers in the gallery, adoring horses, of course, but preferring to do it from an altitude; the waddling, toothless old grooms (what is it in the life of the stable that removes the teeth so surely?); the copers, the subalterns, the yellow-waistcoats, and, oh, the bowlers – all this is very charming; and, enjoying it, one has a new hope for England. It is fashionable to laugh at hunting people, but I see no reason why they should not exist, the same as the rest of us. They look well and they mean well; and it is well known that the fox enjoys the sport as much as any. No, no, so long as there are plenty of good fellows to ride to hounds there is no fear of the country going to the dogs.

Personally, indeed, I have a special sympathy with them, being fond of boats, for I know what quiet pleasure one can get out of a conversation entirely composed of technical terms, especially if someone is listening who doesn't understand them.

George seems to feel this too, though it is my secret belief that he knows as little about hunters as I do.

We approached the chattering crowd in the corner, where the auctioneer was selling "Horace, a bay gelding; makes a noise; good fencer."

"Forty guineas," suggested the auctioneer; "who'll bid forty for Horace for a start?"

No one showed the smallest anxiety to acquire Horace for forty guineas. But two or three men stooped down and stroked the creature's legs suspiciously (it is an unscrupulous trade, and, as often as not, I gather, a horse is fitted with false pasterns).

"Copers," said George. "That off foreleg's filled. By Jove," he went on, sniffing the good stable air, "this brings it all back. For two pins I'd buy a hunter myself. Not had a gallop for years."

"Ten, then," shouted the auctioneer. "Ten guineas bid for Horace – eleven guineas – twelve…"

"It's a nice shiny horse," I said. "Good colour. Kind expression. What sort of noise does he make?"

"Roars," said George. "You listen." Horace was torn from the fond hands of the dealers and trotted roaring down the hall: but the auctioneer roared better.

"Awful nuisance in the field," said George. "He won't fetch much, you'll see. Good action, though. See how he moves his forearms?"

"Yes, he moves those capitally."

"Bit over at the knee, though."

"I don't agree," I said firmly.

"Shouldn't wonder if he forges," said George, well away – "when he's tired, you know. These Irish horses often do. No, I wouldn't give ten pounds for that horse. All right for a lady's hack. No good to hounds, though. Look at his withers."

"Too long, you mean?" I said, hoping I was looking in the right place.

"Not high enough – not for breed. It's not a well-bred beast at all. Look at the tail."

"What's the matter with the tail?" I said wearily, for I had conceived an affection for the handsome Horace and resented the way he was being pulled to pieces.

"The tail," said George patiently, "ought to rise at an angle of forty-five degrees from the point of insertion. This one, you see – "

"George," I said, "you've been reading a book."

"I'm talking about *breed*," said George, flushing at the accusation.

"Tell me," I said, "which pack exactly was it you used to hunt with?"

"Oh, well, if you think you know more about it than I do – " said George, and moved away in a huff.

Horace fetched eighty guineas, and his place was taken by Flying Fish, a brown mare, tubed.

The people about me, who seemed intimately acquainted with the family life and history of every horse put up, discussed with animation the antecedents of Flying Fish, her withers, her tube, her cargo capacity, her owner, his wife, and the amount the mare would fetch – maybe fifty guineas, and dear at that.

After this despised brute was disposed of there was a stir, and we all pressed forward to see the Braddon Rise Hunt horses sold. The first was Boadicea, and in two two's the bidding for Boadicea was up to four hundred guineas. I observed her with interest, a noble and beautiful creature, though not, so far as I could detect, more noble or beautiful than Flying Fish.

The bidding was brisk, but, as usual in modern auctions, deplorably stealthy. It ought to be done, as it is done in old novels, with loud shouts from heated rivals in different parts of the hall. It is not. At last, however, I discovered two bidders, one of whom was faintly cocking his right eyebrow at the auctioneer, while the other was almost imperceptibly twitching his nose. But every time it cost them twenty guineas. There were others also who, with furtive movements of the head or hand, occasionally butted in; but these were the two that mattered.

The excitement was tremendous. I favoured Mr Nose-twitcher; and, fascinated, I watched the auctioneer.

"500 guineas," he boomed. "500 guineas for Boadicea –" Eyebrow was up. "500 – 500 – for a good weight-carrying mare – 540" – Well done, Nose! – "540 – quit now and you lose her – 540 – I'm selling her – 560 – fresh bidder… 580… Against you, Sir."

And his eye met mine. In my excitement I had blinked at him. I had a sudden, terrible suspicion that I was the "fresh bidder."

I looked away, all of a tremble. "600 – 620." Eyebrow was up again. I looked at Nose. "620 guineas bid below" – Oh, go on, Nose! – "640 – 640 – I'm selling her – 640 – a real hard horse – 660 – you lose her – 660 – it's against you – 680 – 680." Brave Nose! Surely he's got it. I glanced with anguish at the auctioneer. "700 – 700 guineas." Oh, Nose! "700 – it's against you." Oh, Nose is done! "700 – Against you – Quite sure? – 700 – I'm sellin' her – 700 – Quite sure? – 700 – last time – 700!" and down came the hammer. "The gentleman over there." Poor Nose!

"Where does *he* hunt, I wonder?" I heard someone say in respectful tones.

Then a man spoke in my ear, also respectful: "WHERE WOULD YOU LIKE THE MARE DELIVERED, SIR?"

Good heavens! I had bought Boadicea! The people near glanced curiously at me. A lady almost smiled at me – the man who had given seven hundred guineas for a horse.

And could I now say, "The fact is, I wasn't bidding. I merely blinked by accident. It's a free country"?

No – a thousand times, no! Already my mare was being led away, the lovely creature. And I followed her proudly to her stall, pursued closely by the official, and a little uncertain what to do with either.

"Well," I said, "she seems pretty snug here. Do you mind keeping her for a day or two? The fact is, my stable's full – crowded out."

"Certainly, Sir."

"Feed her well, won't you? Bran-mashes, and all that."

"Certainly, Sir. And the name?"

"George Rowland, The Albany," I replied without hesitation. After all he *wanted* one. And he can afford it.

The next move was not at the moment clear to me. But heaven smiled, and Mr Nose approached.

"Not thinking better of it, I suppose?" he said, with deference.

"I don't buy hunters for fun, Sir," said I, truthfully enough.

"I was a fool to quit when I did," said Nose. "Got cold feet. Will you take seven-fifty for her?"

"Part with Boadicea! My dear Sir!"

"Eight hundred, then? It's more than she's worth," pleaded Nose.

"Not to me, Sir – not to me; I want a weight-carrier. And I want breed. She's worth a thou' to me – a cool thou'."

(This expression carries weight in any company.)

"Where d'you hunt, then? I don't seem to know your face."

"Philadelphia, chiefly; the Penn country."

"Ah!" said Nose, "Call it nine hundred and split the difference."

"Guineas?"

"Guineas."

"Well, it's a wrench," I said; "but at that she's yours."

"Right," said Nose; "and who shall I make out the cheque to?"

"George Rowland," I said regretfully.

ART

Rail at the Royal Academy if you must, but admit that nowhere else will you hear such jolly conversation. Nor is there another place where a man may see so many of his fellow-countrymen so thoroughly doing their duty. There is about an Academy crowd an air of virtuous bustle, such as one may observe in the apparently futile movements of a number of ants. One feels that in some way not manifest they are all doing a good work, and don't mean to give up.

This comes of buying a catalogue. Sell an Englishman a catalogue and life becomes a sacred duty till he has sucked his money's worth of it. Indeed, if there were no catalogues at the Academy, I fear that many of the pictures would never be seen.

As we entered, a gushing lady swept out of the Sculptural and greeted a female friend who had just arrived.

"Ah, there you are at last!" she said impatiently, as one torn from an absorbing study.

"What's it like?" said her friend.

"Awful," said the other joyously. "I've done the first nine rooms. Haven't seen a thing I liked. Not a *thing*, my dear. Come along; we'll do 10 and 11 and the statues, then we can start again, and I'll show you the best things. You'd better get a catalogue; it's more fun. And you may want to tick some. Not that I've ticked any, so far. Not a thing. My dear, you never *saw* such a – "

Thus encouraged, the other lady bought a catalogue; George also, as a matter of duty. And in this stern spirit he halted firmly before Picture Number One, and set his hand to the plough.

"Number 1, 'Miss Lesley Findlater,'" he announced, "by CECIL JAMESON. Nice girl. That one's 'September,' by ARNESBY BROWN. I've heard of him. He's an RA. Yes, that's rather good." And George gave "September," a good long look. "Number 3, 'Dream Days'; number 4, 'A Happy Family'; 5, 'The Orange Wrap,' by WILL PENN: I've read something about him. 6 is 'An Old Song,' by CONSTANCE REA. 7, That's by – "

"George," I said, "I feel a little faint. Do you mind if I – ?"

"Hard lines, old fellow. Yes, you sit down for a minute. I'll do this room for you."

"Thanks, old man."

I sat down gratefully and watched the busy scene.

Most of them work in pairs, sharing a catalogue. This is well enough where the couple have mutual tastes, supposing there be two such people in the world. But mostly they are husbands and wives, one of whom takes a severe view about pictures, and the other knows what she (or he) likes, and can't think why anyone should want to paint *that* woman. And I have no doubt that many homes have begun breaking up about page 25 of the catalogue.

One such couple were near me. They stood well out in the room, the man preferring to see the pictures at a reasonable range. So I fear he saw little of the pictures on the line, owing to the dear old bodies from Streatham, who must crowd as close as they can, like children round the monkey cage, peering at the face because it looks so real, or simply enjoying their own reflections.

These two were "doing" a portrait which shall be nameless.

"*That's* better," said the man at last. "I like the way the colour's put on. Don't you?" – with the vague gesture without which this kind of remark is incomplete.

"Bad-tempered woman, I should think," said his wife.

"Very likely," said he shortly. "But it's good. The modelling of the cheek – the – the – do you see what I mean?" and he manfully waved his arm again.

"I like the *fan*," said his wife helpfully. "Lovely colour."

"H'm! I'm not sure that doesn't spoil it. Strikes me as insincere," he went on, warming up. "It's not in *tune*, don't you see? The dress is first-rate, the *texture*, the – the *rhythm* of the thing – d'you see what I mean? – but the fan – "

"Just what I want for my Spanish shawl," murmured the lady.

George was now working methodically through the 50's, and I departed stealthily into Gallery III.

One thing I feel most strongly, that all should do their own catalogue work. And I pity most the sad unmarried daughters, who are dragged about as nomenclators by terrific mothers, and seldom have time to glance at a picture themselves. Mere catalogue fodder.

"What's the next, child?"

" 'The Rt. Hon. Sir Frederick George Banbury, Bt., MP,' Mother. By COLLIER."

" 'The Viscount Chelmsford,' Mother, 'GCSI, Viceroy and Governor-General of – ' "

"He was at Winchester with your Uncle John. Fine school. Who did those horses?"

"MUNNINGS, Mother," said the dutiful girl – " 'Brood Mares and Foals.' Are you sure you're not getting tired, Mother?"

"Don't worry about me, child. If you're enjoying it, that's all I care about."

"Yes, Mother; but – "

"What's 227?" said the old martyr.

" 'The Chinese Screen,' Mother, by – "

"What's that portrait? I haven't seen a decent portrait yet. Have *you*?"

"No, Mother. That's an ORPEN, 'Mr – ' "

"Ah, now that's better. That was in *The Times*. Who's that?"

"James Wentworth, Esq."

"Never heard of him."

From South Kensington to Brixton Hill is not so far, after all. At my back, on the same piece of plush, sat three dear comfortable parties, resting, fanning, and thoroughly enjoying themselves.

"Well, my dear, I said to her, I said," remarked one of them, in the smooth and passionless tones of great history: " 'Florence,' I said, 'you've no right to say a thing like that about Mr Derby – not if it was your own husband.' I don't wonder at his taking Ernie's part, I told her, not after the way she's dragged him down. How that man's bore with it so long – ! As I said to her, 'Florence,' I said, 'if you ask *me*, it's a wonder he's not struck you *before*; and now you can summons me if you *like*, but speak out I will!' And with that, my dear, I put on my hat and walked out of the house, believe me or not. And if she was to go down on her bended knees to me, Edie, I wouldn't darken her doors again. As for that baby, it's no good your telling me that's Ernie Pratt's child, because I'll never believe it, if I live to be a hundred. We'd better do a few more now," she continued in the same level tones, "before we get up. You've got the book, Edie. What's this with the castle?"

"We've done that one," said the third lady.

"No, we didn't do that – did we, Edie?"

" 'Between Showers, Arundel,' " Edie read. "It's pretty, isn't it?"

"Arundel," said Ethel, musing. "You go there from Bexhill, don't you?"

"It's Wales, I fancy."

"Well, I could have sworn – Alice, where was it Ernie went that Easter with his uncle – it must be three years now – Littlehampton way?"

"Oh, *that*! Bognor, wasn't it?"

"Bognor – that was it," said Ethel. "Well, you go to Arundel from there. It's a pretty picture, isn't it?"

"Yes, it's sweetly pretty."

"Too blue and green for me," said Alice.

"Well, shall I tick that?" Edie inquired, her pencil poised.

"That's 'The Marchioness Curzon,'" said Ethel dreamily. "She's lovely, isn't she?"

"Yes, she's very lovely."

"*Isn't* she lovely? What did you say, my dear?"

"Shall I tick 'Arundel'?"

"I don't know. Alice, shall Edie tick 'Arundel'?"

"No, I don't think I should tick that," said Alice.

"Tick 'The Marchioness,' anyway, my dear," said Ethel.

"Well, I shall tick both those," said Ethel firmly.

(I don't wish to raise unduly the hopes of the two artists concerned, nor can I explain the full significance of a tick; but let me make it clear that both pictures were duly awarded one.)

A little later, by the merest chance, I stood behind these three dears as they blankly gazed at Sir WILLIAM ORPEN'S satirical "Unknown Soldier" picture.

"Yes," said Ethel at last, "I think that's one of the nicest."

"I shall tick that," said Edie.

A HOT-BED

"Hot-beds," said the man in the big armchair. "Hot-beds of revolution – that's what they are. What time are you lunching, old man?"

"Well, I was just waiting till I felt like it," said the man in the high collar. "No, I don't know what we're coming to. Did you see those statistics of crime in *The Times*?"

It was Sunday at the Rakes' Club, where George had taken me for lunch. And we were discussing the Socialist Sunday Schools.

"I did. But what can you expect? There's the cinema all the evening and these damned schools in the afternoon. What the next generation's goin' to be like I can't think."

"Crime's one thing," said the man with the cocktail, "but Socialism's another." And with that he went in to lunch.

"Breedin' Bolshevists – that's what we are," came from the armchair.

"Ought not to *be* any politics on Sunday," said the high collar. "Have the little devils in an' give 'em a straight talk about the Empire by all means, but – Well, come on, Carruthers; we'll try the new Madeira."

"I hear they drink blood," said the armchair.

An hour or two later George and I were ushered into a hot-bed – a small back room in a grubby Street not many leagues from

Chelsea. At the door, with a reassuring glance, George tapped his side pocket, which I investigated. George had brought a gun.

"You never know," he said darkly.

In the hot-bed were some thirty well-fed children, of all ages from three to thirteen. All wore badges, and one carried a baby.

Mr Tabbery, the teacher – or shall we say, the labourer in the hot-bed ? – led us in. "GOOD AFTERNOON, COMRADES," he boomed in his deep voice, and "*Good afternoon, Comrades,*" piped the children, and at that notoriously seditious word I saw George shiver.

"Which little comrade will recite the text of the month?" asked Mr Tabbery.

"*I* will, Comrade!" said a smug little girl of about nine, jumping up. And she recited rapidly, in the "Eena-meena-mina-mo" manner:

"Love-learning-which-is-the-food-of-the-mind-be-as-grateful-to-your-teachers-as-you-are-to-your-parents."

"That's good, Hettie! And now; Comrades, let us repeat the text together." And the Comrades, standing up, gabbled in unison that same subversive shibboleth, with the exception of the baby-comrade, who gave a low but frankly Republican wail.

Hettie, who wore plaits and a soapy air of importance, was clearly the inevitable star performer of the class. She oozed with righteousness and learning, and never failed to show off when required. As I watched her, my respect for Mr Tabbery increased. Mr Tabbery is a fine honest fellow, with the heroism of the fanatic and the pathetic dignity of the harmless lunatic, both of which one may respect without accepting their expressions of opinion. And for a hard-working man to spend every Sunday afternoon in that dingy little room, inspiring Hettie to love Socialism and the food of the mind, seemed to me the most heroic lunacy I had ever encountered. Harmless? Well, no. The production and encouragement of Hetties is indeed a crime against society.

Still, no one had drunk blood yet.

The Man About Town

"Hand out the books, Hettie," said Mr Tabbery, and, simpering, the dreadful little girl distributed copies of the scarlet Socialist Sunday School Hymn-Book. It contained lyrics by SHELLEY and LONGFELLOW, Mrs HEMANS and one or two bishops. Also, "The Red Flag." And you can take your choice.

An adult Comrade played on a violin an unusually disconsolate tune, and, standing up, we all sang Hymn Number 66:

> I deem that man a nobleman –
> Yea, noblest of his kind –
> Who shows by moral excellence
> His purity of mind.

None sang this louder than the insufferable Hettie. (I claim that it is the worst quatrain in the whole body of English verse.) The rest of the verse ran:

> Who is alike through good and ill
> A firm unflinching man,
> Who loves the cause of brotherhood
> And aids it all he can.

This hymn, every verse of which began with the same line, was evidently aimed at George, and I was greatly afraid that at the last verse he would shoot, if not before. However, he forbore, and we sat down to listen to an address from Mr Tabbery, directed nominally at the children, who paid no attention, but actually at George, who was eagerly reading the redder hymns in the book.

Mr Tabbery made a long and carefully reasoned answer to the attacks of newspapers on the Socialist Sunday Schools, punctuated occasionally with the word "Boys and Girls."

"It is said," he remarked at last, "that we are in the habit of inculcating hatred and class-animosity – Boys and Girls. This is not true, Boys and Girls. Our gospel is the gospel of peace and love. If I had been born the son of a duke, I don't doubt I should have the same outlook on life as he has. We don't *hate* such people – Boys and Girls – we *pity* them. For we believe in the brotherhood of man, and we must not forget that even dukes are human beings like ourselves. I ask you, Boys and Girls, in all these months do you ever remember an occasion on which I have attempted to inculcate hatred or class-animosity?"

There was no answer. The Comrades opened their mouths and gaped at each other; but even the baby was silent.

Then the invaluable Hettie piped up "*No*, Comrade! *Never!*" The situation was saved.

And we rose up and sang in our childish trebles:

> So on we march to battle,
>   With hearts that grow more strong;
> Till victory ends our warfare
>   We sternly march along.

It is an odd thing, but whenever a man talks very big about peace and brotherhood you may be fairly sure that in two minutes he will be singing a song of which every other word is "banner," "battle," or "fight."

However, the children, marched they never so sternly, seemed as sheepish as before, not to say bored; and the only person to behave at all violently was George, who kept discovering red passages in other parts of the book, digging me in the ribs and pointing at them with no little indignation.

For example, while I was singing:

> One heart, one home, one nation,
>   Whose king and lord is love,

The Man About Town

George was pointing at:

> Democracy! Democracy!
>   Our sordid lives take thou in hand,
> Transmute them to a symphony
>   Of organ-music grand...

And another that worried him was the charming lyric:

> Who strives from earliest morn,
>   Who toils till latest night,
> Who brings to others wealth,
>   Ease, luxury, and might?
> Who turns alone the world's great wheel,
> Yet has no right in commonweal?
>   It is the men who toil,
>   The Proletariat;
>   It is the men, the men who toil,
>   The Proletariat.

"If they sing that I shall go out," whispered George.

Personally I would have given a month's salary to hear the little Comrades sing that. Or I would have liked to see them tear the Union Jack to pieces. Or denounce the Constitution. Anything to show that they had a little red blood left in them. But they did not even giggle.

Instead they sang – and now with what gusto! – Hymn 12, the refrain of which is:

> And we practise as we go
>   On the little things we meet;
>   Carrying Granny's parcel for her,
>   Guiding blind men o'er the street;
> Lifting up the fallen baby,
>   Helping mother all we may;

> Thus as little duties meet us
> We perform them day by day.

And, oh! the look on Hettie's face as, loud and clear, she trilled the noble words. Sweet child! I decided once and for all that the suggestion that she drank blood was ill-founded.

The final hymn, I must admit, was pretty red. The tune was the tune of "Auld Lang Syne, and Mr Tabbery announced that at the last verse we should all clasp hands.

The last verse came at last, and it ran:

> And now we'll clasp each other's hands,
> And by the dead will swear
> To keep the Red Flag waving high
> Through all the coming year.

A halt was called, while the children laboriously clutched each other, and with extreme reluctance. Poor Mr Tabbery glanced at George and me, but I regret to say that we both looked the other way, George because he was choking with indignation, and I because I was afraid of giving way to the giggles.

None the less I sang like any Hettie:

> We'll keep the Red Flag waving high
> For Auld Lang Syne.

"By gad, it's awful," said George seriously as we departed.

"It is," I agreed seriously; "it's terrible."

"They'll all grow up Socialists, you know – every one of them."

"They'll all grow up horrid prigs," I said.

THE COURT THEATRE

George and I belong to that distinguished army of men who have been called to the Bar and failed to answer the call; and it is on the doings of such men in the great world that the reputation of the Bar for high intelligence is largely founded. Barristers flatter themselves that they see life in all its aspects – and this is true in the sense that the producers of French farces and drawing-room plays see it. When people liken the Law to good Drama they make a great mistake; but if they likened a distinguished lawyer to a bad dramatist they would in most cases hit the nail on the head. For each, apparently, lives in an entirely fictitious and histrionic world of his own, with a standard of conduct never met with in the world of men; and each makes a great deal of money out of it.

So we do our best to keep our practising colleagues in touch with real life, and now and then take a little lunch with them, and follow it up with a pleasant afternoon in the Chancery Court, listening to some learned men being quietly witty about Contingent Remainders and Executory Devises.

Our last visit was unfortunate. As, of course, you know, one Court, or set of courts, transacts the kindred business of Probate, Divorce, and Admiralty; and there, under the common symbol of the gilt Anchor, the Freedom of the Seas and the Freedom of Divorce are gloriously upheld together. George and I were bent on hearing an interesting case concerning the rights and duties of a Cornish harbour-master in connection with the carcass of a dead whale. We approached a door marked "COUNSEL ONLY," and were admitted under protest. The court was curiously crowded, and a cloud of counsel hung listening intently inside the door. Young barristers are always ready to learn, and evidently the dead whale must have raised some nice legal point to have drawn so many from their work.

A man's voice, deep and vibrant with moral indignation, was heard to say: "DARLING, I AM LONELY WITHOUT YOU. COME BACK SOON…"

"George!" I gasped, "this is the wrong court!"

"Yes, I knew that," whispered George. "That's Mrs Plum in the box." And he gazed with rapture at Mrs Plum.

More barristers came in, and now there was scarce standing-room. Yet this was none of your *causes célèbres*, and occupied next day a bare half-column in the morning papers. Mrs Plum was comparatively unknown to the public. No, the "draw" was Sir Charles Gupp, KC, and on him the attention of the barristers was fixed, their interest in the case being, of course, more purely technical than George's.

Sir Charles was conducting a "deadly cross-examination" of Mrs Plum. Sir Charles specialises in murders and co-respondents, and either he is a superb actor or he has a mind like a sewer; in either case he earns about forty thousand pounds a year.

He said to Mrs Plum:

"Did you write that, Mrs Plum? You did? And on the 15th did you write to your husband in *these* terms: 'Darling Hubby, – Your Tootles misses you. Flo died yesterday, and it's raining hard'? You did? Ha!"

Sir Charles put his foot on the seat, rested his elbow on his knee and weighed his words.

"That was on the 15th. And on the 16th, the day after you sent that affectionate communication to your husband in India, you were *dancing the Foxtrot* with Mr *Spry*?"

"One can't dance the Foxtrot alone," said Mrs Plum.

"Exactly," said Sir Charles, with a very moral light in his eye. "And you and Mr Spry – "

"What is a Foxtrot?" said the Judge.

"Melud," said Sir Charles, "it appears" (appears!) "to be a kind of dance," etc., etc.

"That was at the Palais de Danse, was it not?"

"Yes."

"Yes – I *thought* so."

"What is the Palais de Danse?" said the Judge.

"Melud..." etc., etc.

"Now tell the jury when it was you first met Mr Spry, will you please, Mrs Plum?"

"I first *saw* him on the Underground, two years ago."

"Two years ago! That would be about six months after Mr Plum sailed for India? Ye-es. And what happened when you met Mr Spry on the Underground?"

"I didn't exactly meet him, Sir Charles. He gave me his seat."

"Oh, he gave you his seat, did he? Can you recall your conversation on that occasion?"

"He took off his hat and said, 'Won't you take my seat, Madam?'"

..."*I* see," said Sir Charles in an encouraging tone, as one humouring a child into a confession of naughtiness. "And didn't it strike you as a little *odd*, Mrs Plum, that this man, a Perfect Stranger to you, should come up and *accost* you in this manner? – No? – Oh! – Didn't it occur to you, as a married woman with a husband in India, that that perhaps was the kind of man your husband *would rather you didn't meet*? No? Well – very well," said Sir Charles tolerantly, and paused awhile to let the thing sink in. Then, with challenging severity: "And IN FACT you *did* meet him again? Quite soon?"

"Yes."

"Ah! How was that?"

"At an 'At Home.' It was a coincidence."

"Oh," said Sir Charles, "you met at an 'At Home'? And it was a coincidence?"

"Yes, it was a coincidence. We both knew Mrs Gregor."

"I see," said Sir Charles, nodding kindly, "a coincidence. Tell the jury what happened then,"

"Well, we were introduced, and – and – "

"Yes, Mrs Plum?" said Sir Charles sharply, cocking his head like an exceedingly wicked robin.

"We talked," said Mrs Plum.

"I thought people never talked when they were at home," said the Judge with a benevolent smile, and a roar of laughter shook the court.

"You *talked?*" said Sir Charles in a surprised tone. "Can you recall the subject of *that* conversation, Mrs Plum?" And all of us realised that the previous conversation she had remembered had been somehow very, very damaging.

"No? Very well. What happened then? You went home? Alone? *Not* alone? *I* see. You went home with somebody else. Who was that, Mrs Plum?"

"Mr Spry saw me home."

"Mr Spry? Wasn't that a little remarkable, Mrs Plum? The first time you meet this man – if we exclude the encounter on the Underground Railway – he takes you home from a *party*. Isn't that a little *odd*, Mrs Plum? No?"

"It was a black fog and there were no cabs running." (*Laughter.*)

"O-o-h!" said the righteous man, standing bolt upright. "So Mr Spry took you home in a *fog*, did he? (*Snigger.*) And in the fog I daresay you took his arm, Mrs Plum? (*Snigger.*) Or perhaps he took *yours?*" (*Loud laughter.*)

"Of *course*," said Mrs Plum hotly. "You couldn't – "

"Of *course?*" And now Sir Charles was very stern "Really, Mrs Plum, that is hardly what you mean, is it? The first time you meet this man – "

"It was pitch-*black*," said Mrs, Plum. "You couldn't see your hand in front of your face."

"And you didn't see *his*, eh, Mrs Plum?" snapped the learned wit, and again we roared with laughter, manly, vigorous, refreshing laughter.

"He didn't take my arm," said Mrs Plum; "I took his."

"Ah, it wasn't too dark for *that?*" (*Laughter.*)

Sir Charles, like other KCs, knows how to make the most of a good joke, and this was too good to be left alone.

"You couldn't have seen your hand in front of your face – but, of course, that wasn't where you *put* your hand, was it, Mrs Plum ? – (*Loud laughter.*) – Putting it in front of your face wouldn't have been quite so useful?" (*Laughter*).

"No," said poor Mrs Plum sullenly.

"Or so pleasant? – (*Laughter.*) – So you found this gentleman's arm without much difficulty, Mrs Plum? – (*Laughter.*) – In spite of the fog? – (*Laughter.*) – And how long," said Sir Charles genially, for by now it was quite evident that Mrs Plum was done for – "how long did this agreeable journey continue?" (*Laughter.*)

"About half an hour."

"Ah!" said Sir Charles profoundly.

Oh, when we speak of the Divorce Court as disgusting, let us at least thank Heaven for the spotless mind and personality of Sir Charles Gupp, KC!

THE FIRST NIGHT

George is an inveterate First-Nighter, and is sometimes kind enough to take me with him. George is by now so thoroughly inveterate that wild horses will scarcely take him to a common fourth night or a fiftieth night, or indeed anything short of a 1,000th Performance or an Anniversary Gala Night. Unless he was present at the hatching, the egg does not exist for him.

The nice thing about a First Night is that no one really feels he is at a theatre at all. It is just a jolly family party, broken up by long periods of acting, in the course of which most of the audience are prevented from talking to each other. The very programme girls betray a certain social exaltation not usual in their profession, and murmur "There is *no* charge tonight," with all the pride of a hostess. Only the dramatic critics know very well what they are about, poor fellows. And, of course, the author. – I had forgotten him. But this is often done.

The first night of *The Cabbage Girl*[1] was a brilliant affair. The house was full of the best people, and as we moved to our seats there was a burst of applause from the gallery and the pit. This never happens when I go to an ordinary performance.

"It's Rachel Gay," said George. And there, sure enough, was the famous actress, sitting down in a stall like an ordinary person, only that she miserably failed to look as if she didn't know that everyone was looking at her.

Then a dear old gentleman and his wife crawled over us and sank sighing into their seats.

"That's old Stanger," whispered George with reverence. "He hasn't missed a First Night for thirty years. He spoke to me once. Awfully int'r'stin'. He saw BERNHARDT'S first performance. And he remembers Estelle's last appearance in London. And he's seen The DUSE. And he's seen Lydia Rikitikiteva, and Gretel Hansen, and Maria Dinero, and The Confetti – all of them."

"Then why does he come and see Constance Darling in *The Cabbage Girl?*" I asked.

"I don't quite know," said George. "But of course she's a very old favourite."

" I remember Constance when she was in the chorus," growled old Stanger at this point. "What a draught!"

"Yes, dear," said Mrs Stanger.

" '93. I remember it well. A piece called – called – Damme, I'll forget my own name next. Why don't they shut that door? They can't write plays nowadays."

"No, dear," said Mrs Stanger.

Meanwhile the atmosphere was electric. Haggard young ladies raked each other with field-glasses at close range, and scandal danced merrily from row to row.

About ten minutes after the right time the curtain rose in the peculiarly thrilling manner of First Night curtains and revealed a perfectly empty stage. The audience, eager to encourage, hesitated but a moment and then applauded vigorously. No musical play had ever begun like that before.

"By Gad, that's clever!" said George.

Then eighteen young women in green tights came on, carrying baskets of cabbages,[2] and were loudly applauded by their friends and relations. They danced about the stage, doing exercises with their arms, and singing:

> Joy and gladness
> Banish sadness
>   When the Spring is here.

"The third from the left," whispered George intensely. "Did you ever see such legs?"

"I can't remember," I said. "They remind me vaguely of somebody's – but just whose – "

"Skinny lot of girls," growled Mr Stanger.

The young women then related the life-history of Prince Boris and went off, doing exercises with their legs, and singing:

> Banish sorrow
> Till tomorrow
>   Now the Spring is here.

Minor characters came on, and each in turn was loudly applauded by friends and relations. Mr Stanger turned round and flung a fierce "*S-sh!*" at an innocent lady in the row behind. A man in the gallery booed.

"This'll be a *success*," said George with confidence.

Then Constance Darling came on, and it was evident that she was a woman of many friends and relations. *The Cabbage Girl* part had been specially written for her and she was drawn on in a specially constructed donkey-cart,[3] from which she sang. She was greeted with what is known as a veritable *furore*. The pit and gallery yelled (except for the man in the gallery, who booed), and even the stalls clapped. Only the dramatic critics sat silent and unbending, but for the lady on my left, who scribbled something feverishly on a large pad. As for old Stanger, he quivered with excitement, clapped like a man, coughed violently, wiped his eyes and sank back exhausted, grunting happily, "Not a day older, my dear – not a day. And what a figure!"

"Yes, dear," said Mrs Stanger.

After the First Act the real business of the evening began, and the whole house trooped out to the *foyer* and asked each other what they thought of the play. Several dramatic critics gathered darkly in a corner and, contrary to the popular belief, discussed every play under the sun but *The Cabbage Girl*. The rest of us ventilated our opinions as freely as it is wise to do without having read the papers.

"What do you think of it?" said George.

"Delightful," I said, the well-bred guest.

"So do I. And May Moody's simply *superb!*"

"Isn't she? Superb."

"Hullo, here's Tom. What d'you think of it, Tom?"

Tom shook his head doubtfully. "A bit dull. Lacks *life*, you know."

"Yes, I know what you mean," said George, unabashed. "It might be more lively, certainly."

"And I can't *bear* that terrible girl, May Moody," said Tom.

"Oh, can't you? I rather like her. Of course she's got a rotten part in this."

"She can't sing."

"No, she's not much voice, I know. But she acts so well."

"D'you think so? Of course she's badly produced. That awful wig!"

"Yes, the production's not good," said George with relief. "Well, so long."

"Hullo, George. What d'you think of it?" said another friend behind us.

George pursed his lips. "Not a great deal. A bit lifeless, don't you think? Amusing, all the same. But it's so damned badly produced."

"I think the whole thing's magnificent," said the man. "Suits May Moody so well," and he went away.

During the second Act, whenever Constance was off the stage, Mr Stanger betrayed his enthusiasm for the Theatre in the most curious way. The cabbage girls had been too much for him, and he slowly subsided in his seat, snorting at intervals in clearly audible tones, "Gosh, what a play!" – "And they call that *acting!*" – "The girl's a *stick!*" – "Rubbish!" – "Bosh!" – and so forth. Meanwhile Mrs Stanger, that indefatigable first-nighter, went fast to sleep.

This was before the negroes came on. When that happened Mr Stanger woke his wife and went out.

At the end the curtain rose and fell rapidly a number of times, to a rather tepid applause; Constance Darling beamed and bowed, and the actor-manager beamed and bowed, leading Constance about by the hand and pointing at her, as if we might have missed her. And Constance pointed at the other actors, to show that no part of the credit was hers; and the actor-manager pointed at the conductor, and the conductor pointed at the orchestra; and seven men in evening dress trickled on to the stage, and these all pointed modestly at each other – the Man who Wrote the Dialogue, the Man who Wrote the Lyrics, the Man who Thought of the Plot, the Man who Did the Scenery, the Man who Arranged the Negro Dances, the Man who Did the Lighting, and the Man who Trained the Donkey. Then someone shouted "Author!" and, after a good deal of pointing, we discovered in a corner the little man who had written the rest of the play, bowing timidly at the back of a chorus girl.

Then the Flower Show began, and huge baskets, boxes, and pots of the very largest flowers were heaped upon the stage, almost concealing the men in evening dress. The dear old bouquet is *vieux jeu* to-day, and it will soon be impossible to do floral homage to an actress without having a window-box dragged on to the stage. Constance kissed the salpiglossis and buried her face in the rhododendrons. Then, with difficulty picking up the gardenias, she made a moving little speech in her deep rich voice.

"From the bottom of my heart," she said, gulping a little, "I thank you for your WONDERFUL reception" (at which those who had not clapped very often felt a little guilty, and the man in the gallery booed) "of this WONDERFUL play. Such a WONDERFUL audience…" she faltered. "I don't deserve… I can't tell you… You don't know…from the bottom of my…"

The Man About Town

They dropped the curtain on her.

I put on my coat with a warm sensation, feeling that at least I had given a great deal of pleasure.

1. "Presented by JOHN BAUMANN, by arrangement with Messrs STRING and BEADY, in conjunction with TOM FILTER and HATTIE BLARE, by kind permission of CEDRIC MOON, under the management of STANLEY LAVERSTITCH. Miss MERCY STEIN'S Season. Sole lessees, Messrs MOSS and BLUMBERG." And I do wonder exactly which of them one ought to congratulate about the play.
2. Cabbages by Garrods.
3. The donkey appears by kind permission of Mr John Tattersall. The cart is a Stanley.

THE PERILS OF POLITENESS

George Rowland is a man – and there are many such, who, having a multitude of friends and the faculty of making himself congenial to all sorts of men, supposes that all his friends must be equally congenial to one another. A little Euclid is a dangerous thing.

For years he had been talking to me about his dear friends "the Turners," and striving to arrange meetings – in other words, meals – at which it would at last be revealed to each of the two parties how right George had been in saying that both of them were the best people in the world. But for years we were never all available on the same day.

Then at last, a few weeks ago, the Great Introduction was arranged. George and I were invited together to a little dinner with the Turners at their charming flat in Chelsea. George was as excited about it as a young man introducing a new love to an old one; and by this time, well though I knew George, I confess that I was beginning to feel a faint interest in the Turners myself.

Now it would be idle to pretend that I have more than one white waistcoat; and even my stiff evening shirts are limited in number. Life had been a whirl of pleasure during the previous week, and on going upstairs to dress I found that both the waistcoat and the shirt were at the wash. However, my soft shirts are the envy of Hammersmith; the white tie had seen worse days; the black waistcoat was, after all, a waistcoat; the tailcoat had been specially made for me, and in this picturesque if unconventional combination I rushed out of the house. After all, Chelsea is *so* Bohemian and jolly – they wouldn't mind. Still, for my first meeting with the Turners...

I was late, of course. No man can arrive punctually at a Chelsea home. But, thank Heaven, I had company. Two men in opera hats hustled into the hall of Ormonde Mansions with me, and, squeezing into the lift, we passed upward together, glowering in the usual way.

A tiny cloud, I thought, passed over the brow of my hostess as she greeted me, and I feared that Mrs Turner was perhaps not quite so Bohemian as I had hoped. But there were several ladies present: how right I had been to wear a white tie!

The cloud passed in a moment and she introduced me. "Do you know Mrs Mumble?" she said, and I said straight out that I did not. Then there was a General Mumble, a Sir Charles Mumble, a second Mrs Mumble, Miss Mumble, Captain Mumble, Mr Stanley Mumble, and another Miss Mumble. In fact, all the Mumble family were there as usual. I was introduced as plain Mr Mumble and felt at home at once.

"So glad to meet you at last," I said respectfully to my hostess. "I've heard so much about you."

"That's very kind of you," she said with some restraint.

"But where's our mutual friend?" I asked in surprise, for George was nowhere to be seen.

"He won't be a minute," she said shortly. "A little late – "

"As usual," I said brightly.

"Yes, he's terrible, isn't he?" she said, thawing at last, as if she had only just placed me. Or, more likely, as if she was just beginning to recover from the sight of a friend of the immaculate George clothed in a black waistcoat, tails, and a white tie.

The maid announced that dinner was served, and while Mrs Turner was giving her some last-minute instructions or other our host came in, full of apologies, and hurriedly shook hands all round. He was a charming fellow, with beautiful manners, as

George had often explained, but even he could not keep a tiny film of blankness from his eyes as they rested on me. I must be a terrible sight, I thought.

Evidently, though, he repented at once, for he said most heartily, "So *glad* you could come, Mr – "

"So glad to meet *you* at last," I said with sincerity, for here was clearly the perfect gentleman, especially as I suspected that he had not the faintest idea who I was.

"Any friend of Sibyl's – " he began, but the ladies were trooping out of the door, and all the male Mumbles followed in a bunch.

"I'm afraid we're an odd number," said Mrs Turner in the dining-room. "Will you sit *there*, Mr – ?"

I sat down with alacrity on the left of the younger and more beautiful of the Misses Mumble, and, with less alacrity, on the right of the General, to whom I attributed a complete lack of sympathy with Bohemianism.

"Rotten staff-work, Sibyl," said Mr Turner playfully.

"Well, I like *that*!" she exclaimed, with a reproachful glance at her lord, at which he looked puzzled, and glanced quickly at me and very quickly away again. At which it crossed my mind that George's estimate of the Turners' anxiety to meet me had perhaps been exaggerated. So like George. Meanwhile, where *was* George? Not coming after all, it seemed. That was like him, too. He had flung a perfect stranger at the Turners' heads, made their party an odd number, and not come himself; and the Turners, with superb politeness, were making the best of it, and in spite of my clothes. Meanwhile…

"Have you read *Darkness*?" Miss Mumble was saying very sweetly.

What a delightful girl! What admirable soup!

Darkness led to BARRIE. And BARRIE to favourite authors. And so to KIPLING. And she had been to India. But no, she had not met my cousin Smith out there. All the same the world *was* a small place, wasn't it? She remembered once…

What a good dinner! What fish!

The conversation became general. I told the story of LORD CHARLES BERESFORD and the American. A huge success. What charming people! George was right. What wine!

The conversation became particular.

Had I read *Darkness*? No, I hadn't read *Darkness*. Yes, she remembered I'd said I hadn't read *Darkness*. She hadn't read *Darkness* either. But Mrs Graham had read *Darkness* and said it was good. Mrs Graham was her greatest friend. They had yachted together. And then, of course, it came out that all her passions and enthusiasms were mine – Sailing, and Gardening, and the Drama, and Singing in the Tube. It was amazing. And Mrs Graham was the same.

"What Mrs Graham, is that?" I asked idly, capturing a new potato. I felt that I had known the Turners for years.

"*This* one – Sibyl."

"You mean Mrs *Turner*?"

"No, I mean Mrs *Graham* – our hostess."

I put the potato back.

"Oh," I said, in a cold sweat, but marvellously calm. "Then which is Mrs Turner?"

"There's no Turner here that I know of. There are some people called Turner in the flat below, though. Perhaps you're thinking of them?"

"It's just possible," I said. "As a matter of fact – "

"Sibyl asked them to come tonight, but they're giving a party themselves. Nice people! It's funny you haven't met them."

"It is," I said. "Quite funny. By the way, you might tell me what I ought to do"; and in the strictest confidence I explained the situation.

Miss Mumble giggled stealthily for some time. Then she said, "You can't do anything. You can't get up and make a scene in the middle of *this* party, and you can't arrive in the middle of the other party. You'd better stay here and brazen it out. The Grahams won't discover till you've gone, because each of them thinks the other one invited you. If you go now you'll only make a fool of – of them. In fact, I think it's your *duty* to the Grahams to stay."

"How true," I said. "And a man's duty – "

"Of course," she went on, "you might slip out when the ladies retire."

"I shan't go till then, anyway," I said with some decision.

It was a very jolly party. After the ladies had gone the General talked amusingly and ceaselessly; and after that Miss Mumble sang; and no awkward questions were asked, and we were all great friends. I thrust the Turners out of my mind altogether.

At about ten a lady and gentleman and a young man came in.

"Oh, Sibyl," said the lady, "we thought we'd look in for a few minutes after all. Our principal guest never turned up."

"Hullo, Pat!" said the insufferable George.

"Hullo," said I. "How d'you do, Mrs Turner. So we meet at last."

THE PARLIAMENT OF MOTHERS

"Tea on the Terrace," said George. "Come On."

"Jolly!" I said. "But how?"

"I was at school with our Member," said George loftily.

George and I read the evening papers regularly, so we know what to think of Parliament. And we approached it jauntily, with due contempt.

But we were soon put in our place. The very smell that emerges from the entrance a soapy, cathedral smell – is enough to subdue a scoffer. And the vast Policeman at the door immediately made it clear that this was a place to be respected. In low, cathedral tones we told him that we wished to see George's Member, and he wafted us on into the austere and soporific smell. If we still had any lingering doubts of the dignity of Parliament, they were removed by the size of the Policeman about twenty yards farther on, to whom we whispered that we wished to see George's Member. We crept forward fearfully, half drunk with the smell, and by the time we had reached the Third Policeman we had all but abandoned the idea of seeing George's Member. However, we stuttered nervously that we wished to see George's Member, and were admitted to the Central Hall.

At the entrance to the passage which leads to the House of Commons stand the Fourth and Fifth Policeman. For majesty, sagacity, bulk, and (when they unbend) geniality, the House of Commons' Policemen have no equal among the official classes;

and these two beat all records. To them we said simply that we wished to see George's Member. They gave us two green cards, on which we wrote that we wished to see George's Member. "Object of Visit" I left blank. George wrote "Tea on the Terrace," but he rubbed it out for fear of the Fourth Policeman. The cards we gave to the Fifth Policeman, who gave them to a distinguished gentleman in evening dress, probably the Sergeant-at-Arms. Then we melted guiltily into the cloud of constituents, feeling like men who have deliberately tampered with the British Constitution.

In the Central Hall the dignity of Parliament is never for a moment relaxed. The Sixth and Seventh Policeman see to that. We stood with the other constituents by the barriers, hushed and reverent; and George was in constant trouble with the Sixth Policeman for standing in the wrong place.

An hour and a half passed. The statues of Mr GLADSTONE, of LORD RUSSELL, LORD GRANVILLE, and LORD IDDESLEIGH became increasingly distasteful, and only the hope of tea sustained me. Now and then a Member swept busily down the passage, and the Fourth Policeman, in a voice like Rhadamanthus', boomed out his name; and a wretched clot of constituents shuffled forward, cringing and broken, as if they half expected their Member to strike them in the face or put them in the Tower. This is an odd spectacle when you think with what contempt and bravery, not to say rudeness, they treat their Members when they catch them in their constituencies at Election time. In the Central Hall the constituent is a very different creature.

But there, the Members soon put them at their ease; and it did one good to see it.

The hearty handshakes, the beaming smiles of welcome – like mothers greeting a long-lost child, like hens gathering their chicks. And now with what pride and joy the faces of those constituents were lighted up as they realized that, after all, their Member vividly remembered them, had been anxiously looking forward to this visit, and was now proposing to give them Tea. Tea!

Ah, happy ones! George's Member is no gentleman, though he was motherly enough. When he arrived at last, he made no reference to tea. What he did say was, "Look here, old fellow, you'd like seats in the Gallery, wouldn't you?"

"Rather," said George, but without passion.

"Delighted," I murmured.

"Well, it won't be easy," said George's Member, "but I'll see what I can do. You wait here."

"Don't bother, *please*," I said; but he had gone.

I took George behind the statue of Mr GLADSTONE and said a few quiet words.

About half an hour later, famished and worn, we found ourselves being handed along a passage by a chain of flunkeys, venerable men in evening dress, each of whom had the aspect of a statesman of the old style; and, under the lowering eye of the most venerable of them all, we signed our names in a great book, and undertook to be of good behaviour and make no disturbance in the Gallery. By that time my spirit was absolutely broken, and I should as soon have thought of making a disturbance in the Gallery as I should think of interrupting a sermon. As for George, for the first time I saw him cowed.

Yet another flunkey in the Gallery, with a hissing menace in his voice, ushered us into a seat. We sat down, scarce venturing to breathe. True, at the moment it was a little difficult to understand the stealth and silence which possessed us all up there; for from the Chamber below there came up to us a loud buzz of conversation. A number of gentlemen, too, whose appearance was refreshingly commonplace after the oppressive distinction of the flunkeys, were walking about the Chamber, or lolling back and talking to each other, or quietly studying documents. One gentleman was standing up and, to judge from the movements of his lips and hands, was making a speech; but he did not seem to disturb the conversation of his colleagues in any way, and in general there was a complete absence of that stiffness and restraint which I had noticed in other parts of the building. That air of sedulous maternity, that careful dignity, had dropped from the Members; here at least they could relax, and they were making the most of it.

But nobody else. George turned to me and whispered some remark about an elderly baronet who sat high on the back benches in a top-hat...

"S-S-S-S-S-ST!"

A terrific hiss of rebuke smote us in the back of the neck from the horrified official at the door. We shrivelled up.

The baronet sat with his eyes closed, and his top-hat tilted, like a gentleman asleep. But it was clear that he at least was following the speech with attention. For suddenly he opened his eyes and said, "SHUT UP!" in tones of extraordinary ferocity. Then he closed his eyes again and appeared to sleep. But at intervals he woke up and snapped "SIT DOWN!" and sometimes "STUFF!" or "FLAPDOODLE!" In their general sense his contributions to the debate were admirably consistent.

A gentleman on the other side occasionally retorted with the words, "You DIRTY DOG!" "BLACKGUARD!" or "SOT!" but the debate continued its even course, and the speaker placidly went on with his speech in perfectly inaudible tones.

When he sat down, an action which caused no perceptible excitement, a mild-looking gentleman on the Front Bench rose up and said haltingly:[1]

"I am sure that the sense of the House is that all sections of the House will agree with reference to the Clause which we are discussing that it is not a Clause which any section of the House would wish to become part of the Bill pending the findings of the committee which, as the House is aware, is now discussing the subject-matter of this Clause which we are discussing, and which has been put down by the Honourable Member for Byles; and may I add with reference to the remarks which were made by the Honourable and Gallant Member for Kilmannan and Bogg with reference to that Committee, that when he said that that Committee was not a Committee which ought properly to consider the subject-matter of this Clause indeed, I think he went so far as to say that that Committee was not a Committee, which – "

"IT'S A LIE!" cried an Honourable Member passionately. And A Painful Scene began.

The Honourable Baronet opened his eyes and said "SKUNK!" emphatically.

"Skunk, yourself!" was the ready retort. "Mr Speaker, Sir, is it in order for the Honourable Member for Carraway to call me a skunk?"

The Speaker rose, and was understood to be giving his opinion about this; meanwhile the debate continued.

"He's a dirty dog!"
"What about you?"
"You're the worst!"
"Come outside and I'll show you!"
"Blackguard!"
"Fish-face!"
"Capitalist!"
"Toad!"

The place was now in an uproar, and about this point George ventured to address me again.

"I see *now*," he shouted, above the din, "why – "

"You mustn't talk." I yelled. "You'll disturb the debate."

"I'll risk it," he shouted back. "I see why they have to be so careful about the behaviour of the Gallery. After all, *someone* must set an example. CAN YOU HEAR ME?"

"YES," I bawled. "WHAT THEY WANT DOWN THERE IS TWO OR THREE OF THOSE POLICEMEN!"

1. This is not how the speech is reported in *Hansard*, but this is what, in fact, he said.

"LE BOXE"

Boxing is a noble sport, for those who have the right kind of nose. For myself, I believe strongly that every man should be able to defend himself at need, but the chances are that the other man will always have a more suitable nose, and be even more capable of defending himself than I. Better surely to practise the art of writing my enemy a nasty letter. On a half-sheet of notepaper I will undertake to make any pugilist sit up.

I imagine that in the days of Imperial Rome, as they watched the efforts of an Early Christian to cope with a tiger, the audience used to whisper to each other that every man should be able to defend himself against a tiger at need, and would then go home happy. Making no comparisons, of course, I wish that some of the cultured people and distinguished authors who flock to the Big Fights, and in their drawing-rooms grow lyrical about the Beauty of the Human Form and the Human Form of CARPENTIER in particular – I wish they would visit the Arena one night, and see boxing as it is done in South-East London three times a week, and done by a number of unusually ugly men in a very grubby place; and tell us what they think of it.

Still, when I saw the veteran and practising pugilists stroll in and sit down defiantly in the front rows, I began to understand the aesthetic enthusiasm of Culture for the sport. Nothing shows off the beauty of the human form like a cauliflower ear, or a nose flattened into a small knob, or a jaw like a mule's, or a skin like raw leather with pretty little blotches on it. The shape of these heroes would have put the most modern of our sculptors to shame.

The walls were thickly placarded with "BETTING STRICTLY PROHIBITED," which I was glad to see, not having this particular vice. I can't afford it.

Two nearly naked men of great strength and repulsive appearance entered the ring for a six-round contest. There were a few conventional cheers, and then the air was thick with the subdued cries of persons anxious to bet with friends in other parts of the house.

The man in the front row before me had a curious technique. Like most of us he wore no collar; he looked as if he had never possessed twopence in his life, and he was called Joe. He took a cursory glance at the two combatants, turned round in his seat, pushed back his cloth cap and, addressing apparently some unseen deity above us, remarked in low tones:

"I'll bet two 'alves."[1]

Nothing happened.

"I'll bet two 'alves," he said again.

The bell rang. The first round was over.

During the interval Joe took a good look at the combatants, who were having water poured into them out of bottles and generously spitting it into buckets When they resumed the fight, he turned his back on them again and murmured placidly aloft: "I'll take six ter four."

Nothing happened.

"Tom," he said, more loudly, "I'll take six ter four."

Then I discovered Tom, who stood in the gallery, a commanding figure, and surrounded by friends. How Tom was to discover which of the combatants Joe wished to back was not clear to me. Nor, I think, was it clear to Tom. For during the next three rounds there proceeded an elaborate bargaining, conducted chiefly by secret signs, Joe holding up his fingers and nodding emphatically, and Tom shaking his head with equal emphasis.

Meanwhile under the brilliant lights the boxers fought on almost unobserved, for the talented Tom was carrying on similar negotiations with half the house. During the last round, however, he came to some sort of an understanding with Joe.

Joe turned to the friend beside him.

"Poor fight, ain't it?" he said.

"You're right."

During the next fight, which diverted many of the audience from their business, the traditional chivalry of the ringside was seen. There came in a lusty looking man called Ed Skinner, and a very skinny one called Al Jones, who was greeted with incredulous laughter, but sat down confidently, crossing his legs.

" Bert," said Joe pontifically, "if ever you see a man cross 'is legs in the ring, *back the other feller.*" And, turning round, he said, "Tom! I'll bet two 'alves." And negotiations began again.

In the meantime, Al, the skinny one, the leg-crosser, was knocking the strong one all round the ring with the most accomplished ease. Before the end of the round Ed had fallen down twice; his face was the colour of raw meat; his ears were more shapeless than before, and he was clearly in the extremity of distress. The sporting crowd, who had so lately laughed at Al, now yelled their derision of the unfortunate Ed. " 'Old *that* one!" they jeered as Ed received a terrific blow on the nose; and "After 'im, Al! Keep it there, boy!" And when Ed, in spite of all, smiled a plucky but sickly smile Bert remarked with some venom, "Go on, Al! Take that smile off 'is face!"

Joe, however, asserted passionately that Al was very far from fighting fair; and others who had backed Ed stood up for fair play in the same fearless manner. And the father of Ed, who was standing near, with wild cries encouraged his son to further efforts.

" 'Ave a *go*, son!" he cried plaintively, dancing on his toes, "Go in an *'it* 'im!" and, as Ed feebly tried to defend himself from a shower of blows, "Wot er yer *afraid* of? 'It 'im with yer *left*, boy! Wot er yer *afraid* of?"

"Reminds me of my uncle in the War," said George.

After two rounds the referee stopped the butchery of Ed.

"None of yer ding-dong struggles for me," said Bert. "I like to see a man 'ammered. 'Oo do you bet 'ere?" he went on as the next couple appeared.

"I've been carved out of a quid," said Joe gloomily. "Let's go an' 'ave one."

"Not yet," said Bert, who had backed Al and would presumably have to pay for the refreshment. "Now 'ere's a well-built kid if you *like*."

A hush had fallen upon the house. South London is as susceptible to Beauty as the Albert Hall, and one of the new boxers was a very handsome lad. Slight and smaller than his thick-eared opponent, he obviously could not win, but he should go far to becoming a Carpentier, if he can keep his looks. When he was banged on the nose not a man jeered at him. Such is the power of Beauty.

"Yus, 'e's a nicely built kid," said Joe judicially.

"You're right."

"Well-made, 'e is."

"Yus, I call 'im a very well-built kid. 'Oo do you bet?"

"I shan't bet 'ere," said Joe shortly.

Such is the power of Beauty.

The fight was declared a draw.

Such is – But no.

The big fight of the evening was between "Soldier" Smith, Plaistow (a Guardsman, I imagined – probably a VC), and Bud Peters, Walthamstow. George and I had a little bet, for the fever had me. I bet George that Joe would lose his bet, whatever it was. I had a quiet faith in Joe.

Joe said confidently, "I bet the Soldier. 'E was in the War. Tom! *Tom!* will you give me two quid ter one the Soldier?" Tom shook his head.

"Will you give me two ter one the Soldier, Bert?"

"I should think I would an' all," said Bert. " 'E's only a air-mechanic when all's said."

My faith in Joe mounted.

"Am I on, then? Right," said Joe.

The Soldier was knocked out in the second round. Joe was carved out of another quid. And I had earned one.

"An' now," said this man of wealth, "we'll go an' 'ave one. Tom! *Tom!* Am I on the 3.30 termorrer? *Love-Lies-Bleedin'*? Am I right? At sevens? Right! Come on, Bert, I'm on." And the two millionaires departed.

So did we.

"Fine sport," said George.

"Yes," I said "I don't know where I've seen such betting."

---

1. Half-sovereigns.

A FEW SAMPLES

Did you notice it – that peculiar phrase in a speech of the Right Honourable – , Minister of – , the other day? He was reported to have said that "The financial situation of the country at the present time is very smooth and of an excellent nutty flavour." A curious utterance – and I happen to know how it came to be attributed to him, for George Rowland was at that time his Private Secretary (unpaid), helped with his speeches, and handed the notes of them to the Press. And this was how it happened.

Every two or three months I lay down a few bottles of port – by the pair. I buy wine by the pair because my cellar, consisting of the bottom shelf of the grocery cupboard, will not accommodate any very considerable hogshead or bin. And as a rule I buy it in this way.

Entering my wine-merchant's (for I would have you know that I have a merchant of my very own) I say politely, "I want some nice port, please."

"Certainly, Sir," says the immaculate Mr Jones. "A dozen – or two?"

"A bottle, or two," I correct him gently.

Mr Jones looks at my clothes, remarks curtly, "Bring a couple of the Armistice, Tom," and disappears.

Tom at last produces two rather new-looking bottles, sealed with rather fresh-looking sealing-wax, and says, "This is our Armistice port, Sir."

I say firmly, "Are you sure this is a *nice* port?" He says firmly, "Yes, Sir. I am sure it will suit you very well."

Then I know that I have got a good thing; and I carry it home by the Underground Railway.

When George had dined with me once or twice he asked me, rather rudely, what chemist I went to for my wine. When I told him "Jones & Jones," he said, "Good Heavens! That's where my chief gets *his!* They ought to give you something better than *this!* I shall have to take you there myself."

He took me there. He took me there one Monday after lunch. He stalked superbly past Mr Jones, and sat down superbly in an inner sanctum, with the air of a man about to buy a barrel of Waterloo brandy. Mr Jones came in after us, and inquired politely after the Minister's health. The change in him was extraordinary. He fawned.

George said, "My friend here proposes to give a dinner – in fact, a series of dinners; and he wants some *really* good wine. Now what about some sherry?"

"Certainly," said Mr Jones. "Would you be taking it with the fish – or *before* the dinner?"

"Both," said George grandly.

"Then I can recommend *this*," said Mr Jones. So saying, he seized a bottle from a shelf, madly removed the cork, and poured out three full brown glasses. "A rich old-fashioned wine, Mr Rowland," he remarked with emotion, as he rolled a little round his tongue, and gazed profoundly at George. George rolled half a glassful round his tongue, and gazed profoundly at Mr Jones.

"Too dry," he said with contempt, and drained his glass to the dregs.

Mr Jones was not daunted. "I wonder how you would like our No. 380?" he said; and he presented each of us with a beautiful catalogue in the manner of an author giving away his own works. No. 380 was described as "dark in colour and very intense from age in cask. Has a markedly vinous flavour."

"Very well – open a bottle of that," said George graciously. I gasped, but Mr Jones obsequiously obeyed.

When it came, George first sipped it suspiciously, then rapidly emptied his glass, at which Mr Jones smiled to himself with conscious pride. "A very generous wine," he murmured. "Very rich and generous in character." What was my horror (and Mr Jones') when I observed a look of loathing pass over my friend's face, as if he had just taken some nauseating drug!

"Not dry enough," he snapped. "Not *nearly* dry enough! Don't you agree?"

I hastily agreed – though indeed I was still toying with my first glass.

Mr Jones winced, and offered a third brand of sherry, which was smooth, clean on the palate, and medium dry: but George waved him aside. "Chablis," he said, imperiously. "My friend always gives oysters at his dinners." George knows perfectly well that I never gave away an oyster in my life. I opened my mouth to protest, and received a violent kick on the ankle. I was silent.

Tom was sent downstairs for a special Chablis, "very flavoury and full in style, and of great vinosity." When he had gone George murmured reflectively, "I am not sure that I wasn't *wrong* about that second sherry, after all, Mr Jones. Let me try it again, will you?"

Mr Jones beamed. "I *thought* you'd say that," he said, as he poured out about three-shillings' worth. "This is a wine you can come back to *again and again*. And we are practically giving it away. What we are asking for it will scarcely pay for the *bottling*."

"This shop is really a sort of charity, you see," murmured George to me. This seemed to me to be no more than the truth, and I thought that it ill became George to be ironical about it.

This time he licked his lips, and said: "A pleasant wine – but too *rich*. My friend likes a sherry with rather less *body* in it – *don't* you?" I duly made a vague murmur deprecating body in sherry. Mr Jones regarded me with ill-concealed contempt.

Events then moved very rapidly. It took George a glass and a half to make up his mind about the Chablis. Of this Mr Jones remarked: "It would be difficult to find a more charming little wine than this." But the things George said about it were quite violent.

After that he had a go at some of the more expensive champagnes. It was at the second champagne – the 1906 – that it crossed my mind that George was losing his reserve of manner. Of this wine the catalogue said that it had developed strikingly with age in bottle, and the roundness now shown makes it none too dry. The meaning of this escaped me (in any case I was still at the Chablis), but George tossed off a glass, and holding it out for replenishment, shouted cheerfully, "It's too *round*, Mr Jones! It's much too *round!* By Gad, it's not fit to *drink!* Give me some more!"

Mr Jones' beam had become a little watery by this time, but he complied, and we passed on to the port.

I have but a hazy memory of what followed, but I know that even Mr Jones became a little excited over the various ports George sampled (I say George, for by this time I was laps and laps behind). And I remember Mr Jones saying with great reverence: "Now *this*, Mr Rowland, is something *really* choice. Soft and full – good body – and with a rich plummy flavour – "

And then George burst into song. Waving his glass, and to a tune which was only faintly reminiscent of an air from the *Beggar's Opera*, he sang:

> Fill every glass,
> For wine is plummy, and clean on the palate,
> Smooth, and round,
> Vinous, and soft

> From age in cask,
> Fill every glass...

And I suppose that at that point we left the shop. I only remember vaguely that Mr Jones said something about my making a purchase, which seemed to me to have no point at the time. And I have a hideous, hideous suspicion that I replied carelessly: "Oh, send me a couple of your Armistice port, Mr Jones."

But I clearly remember navigating George back to Whitehall, still humming:

> Fill every glass,
> For wine is plummy, and clean on the palate...

And I know very well why the Right Honourable — is reported to have told his constituents that the financial situation of the country at the present time was very smooth, and of an excellent nutty flavour.

NEVER AGAIN

OR, PEOPLE I DON'T PLAY GOLF WITH TWICE

1

JENKINS

Strictly speaking, of course, there are very few people I do play golf with twice. I do not often have a second chance. Nevertheless, one has one's pride, and there are still golfers whom I regard with contempt.

There is, for one, the Hare-and-Tortoise-Combination man, and Jenkins is the best specimen I have seen.

You know him, of course. He has not long taken up the game, and has just reached the stage of earnest pessimism, but not the stage when one loses faith in the universe. He still takes 12 strokes for the first hole and 69 for the first 7, but he counts them as carefully as he did when he began.

Nay, more carefully. For he has now a standard. Once, it seems, he went round the whole course in 182, and he still clings to the fantastic notion that one day he may beat that score. By a happy chance he has a complete record of that round, hole by hole, and every round he plays now is just a red-hot struggle against that personal Bogey of his own. This contributes largely to the charm of playing with him.

The only time I played with him I took good care to breakfast early and get away before the crowd. We started about half-past eight in the morning, and for the first seven holes we had the course to ourselves. Jenkins halted on every green and got out his spectacles, pencil, and a bundle of old cards, and did mathematics. It was a warm morning, so I was quite content. I like a quiet walk round the links.

At the seventh I holed my approach for 8 – a pretty shot. Jenkins was on the green, but he had played 11 and was a long way off. He got out his cards and began adding.

"Sixty-six," he said at last with suppressed excitement. "If I get down in 2 I shall be one better than yesterday for the 7 holes." And one could see the man bracing his muscles as he took out his putter.

Just then there came a huge bellow out of the distance and, looking round, I saw two large gaunt men leaning on tremendous brassies in attitudes of impatient fury.

"Come on," I said to Jenkins; "it's *my* hole, anyway."

"No, no," he said, almost piteously; "I must put this down."

And put it down he did – in four carefully played putts.

"Seventy," he said sadly, as I hustled him off the green. "That's bad. I did those holes in 67 once."

"We'd better let these fellows go through," I said nervously; "they're scratch men." Whenever I see a high man in baggy breeches behind me my instinct is to lie down at once and let him fire over my body, rather than delay him for the fraction of a second. But Jenkins would not have it. I had not reckoned with the Hare portion of his complex personality. He regards golf as a kind of race, and can't bear to let anybody go past him. He feels that he is losing caste.

So we went on. Somehow or other we scrambled through the eighth hole, which is a short one; but while Jenkins was working out his averages on the green there were no fewer than three couples of long gaunt men leaning on their irons on the tee and shaking their fists at us in a discouraging way.

The ninth was a long hole, and Jenkins still refused to surrender our lead. I saw that we should have to run for it. Jove, how we ran! Back and forth we trotted across the fairway, in and out of bunkers, over walls, and into ditches, just giving our balls a feverish dig in the stern and galloping after them again.

It was no good. Hockey was never my game. The long gaunt men marched down upon us with the easy gait of tigers; and at last I putted my ball down a rabbit-hole and, crying wildly "I've lost my ball!" lay down exhausted.

"Play another," cried the eager Jenkins.

"I haven't got another," I lied, down-and-out.

A long time I lay there, watching against the sky an endless procession of tigers trooping past triumphant. Jenkins fretted at my side, losing caste perceptibly, and working out his chances of doing the hole in under 16.

At last, when there was not a man to be seen behind us, I consented to proceed. At the tenth I was 10 up and 8 to play, and it was one o'clock.

"Well, I had all the luck," I said cheerfully. "What about some lunch?"

"One hundred and two," said Jenkins as one in a dream; "that means that I've only to do a few eights and nines to beat my record. Think I can do it?" Well, one has always a certain sneaking respect for the fanatic, and lunch at the clubhouse is an expensive meal. We went on.

We still had the course to ourselves, and Jenkins took his time. The farther we went the longer he addressed his ball, so long that the club sheep would come and graze in front of him while he did it. First he would make six or seven determined passes in the direction of the hole, as if to warn the sheep that he meant business. Then he placed his club firmly behind the ball, and left it there for a long time, thinking. Then he made four or five little threatening movements at it and raised his club above his head, looking very fierce. One felt that he was about to strike the ball. Then he noticed the sheep. When he had shooed them away he started again. About half-past three we sighted the eighteenth green. "A hundred and eighty-seven," said Jenkins sadly as we staggered off it. "A close thing."

"Bad luck," said I. "But cheer up. If you'd only taken six strokes less you'd have beaten your record."

"That's true," said Jenkins brightening. "Do you think I ought to get a baffy?" he went on anxiously.

"What you want is one of those automatic adding machines," I said.

We had a painful tea.

2

SPICER

Then there is Spicer, or The Man Who Knows Exactly What I'm Doing Wrong.

Fortunately my game with Spicer was a Mixed Foursome, and Spicer was playing with his wife. Nothing else, I think, saved Spicer from a dreadful end. For when he is playing with his wife he has little time to devote to other people; and for some reason Mrs Spicer refrains entirely from striking him with niblicks or pushing him over the cliff at the twelfth, as I should certainly have done if our match had been a single.

And yet how happily we started! A warm and mellow evening, and my drive went skimming over the first bunker as straight and swift as an old swallow migrating out of England on a cold wet day in August.

"Good shot," said Spicer grudgingly. "I didn't think you'd hit that. You dropped the right shoulder."

"Oh!" said I carelessly, for my heart was full.

My next shot was a dream. But "Slow back – slow *back* man," said Spicer sadly, while the ball was yet in the air. "You didn't deserve *that*," he added, as it came to rest within three feet of the hole.

"Thank you," I said with dignity, for after two shots such as those I didn't propose to take advice from any old golf-bore, though he might have three wooden clubs, a Sammy and a jigger, and a patent ball-sponge in his pocket.

But none the less, when it was my turn to drive again, the canker had got me. "Slow back," I said to myself, as I waggled at the ball. "No doubt the old fool was right. Slow back – and for the Lord's sake keep that right shoulder in the sky. *We*'ll show him!"

And of course I hit the ball ten yards.

"I expected that," said Spicer smoothly. "You were standing right in front of it."

After that my game when to pieces. I could do nothing right. And Spicer, having destroyed me for the day, turned his attention to his wife. Mrs Spicer plays very badly, with a steady, methodical, consistent badness that commands one's admiration. She has played for ten years and she knows, and Spicer knows and everybody knows, that she will never play any better. Yet she plays. She plays with Spicer. She is heroic.

The newspapers tell us that in America women seek divorces because their husbands go off and play golf without them. The crying need of English womanhood is some redress against the husbands who force their wives to play golf *with* them.

Mrs Spicer is a born fool, no doubt. Her ball lay about fifteen yards from a stone wall. After fingering doubtfully every club in her collection, she threw a timid glance at Spicer, who stood silent as a Sphinx, and took out her niblick. Spicer waited till she had done three preliminary waggles, and then:

"Take your mashie!" he snapped.

Mrs Spicer jumped like a shot doe and took out her mashie. After a long preparation she hit the ground very hard and the ball very gently.

"Lifting your head again," groaned Spicer, savagely digging the ball out of a rut. "How do you *expect* to get over if you lift your head?"

"But I *didn't* expect to get over, Cuthbert," bleated the poor lady. "You know I *never* expect to get over *anything* with my mashie."

"Then why didn't you use your niblick?"

"But, Cuthbert, you *told* me – "

"It's no good arguing. You dropped the right shoulder, and that's all there is about it."

"But, Cuthbert, I thought you said I *mustn't* lift the right – "

"I said you mustn't lift your head," roared Spicer. "Now try this. Take your mashie. No, take your niblick – no, not that one – your mashie-niblick – here, *this* one," said, Spicer, scattering her clubs like the cut corn upon the ground. "It's a perfectly simple shot. Just hit your ball two yards to the right of that rabbit-hole – not too hard and not too soft. Keep your eye on the ball and let the club come right through. Don't cramp that left elbow. Slow back, right shoulder up, keep that little finger tight, and you'll be all right. There's nothing in it."

Mrs Spicer approached the ball, trembling like a leaf, and miraculously hit it a full twenty yards.

"Um," said Spicer, not unkindly, "but you must keep that right heel down."

"*Dear* Cuthbert!" whispered his wife a little later, with tears in her eyes. "He *is* so patient with me. I know I'm terribly stupid at it, but it *is* difficult to think of so many parts of one's body at the same time, *isn't* it? It makes me feel quite *naked*."

When she next had to drive, for a moment or two I feared for Mrs Spicer's reason. She waggled at her ball for a long, long time, so long that the whole party had the fidgets, and when it seemed that she was really about to aim a blow at it at last she did no such thing, but rested her club on the ground and stood like one in a trance – only we saw that her lips were moving.

"Right shoulder up – head down," I caught faintly. She was repeating, like some magic incantation, the very last edition of Spicer's instructions.

Finally her brow puckered and, gazing downwards, she made curious motions with her feet; then, coming out of the trance, she murmured softly. "*What* was it you said about the right heel, Cuthbert? Was it *down* or *up* it had to be?"

"Oh, hit it anyhow!" said Spicer savagely.

Thus encouraged, his lady walked right away from her ball, and, walking back again, just hit it, anyhow. The ball flew fair and far, a long way down the centre of the course, a superb shot.

"Oh, Cuthbert, *isn't* that a lovely one?" she cried, flushed with joy. "*Look* what a way it's gone!"

"Yes, it went well enough," growled Spicer; "but, good Heavens, you don't call that *golf!*"

Poor Mrs Spicer! She won't try that again.

3

SIMPSON

Then, of course, there is the Fussy and Academic Golfer, who objects to smiling on the green and knows by heart that vast body of customs, rules, traditions, and by-laws which compose the whole ritual of Golf.

Men had warned me about Simpson; so before we set off I slipped a small copy of *The Rules of Golf* in my pocket, thirty-three pages, complete with index.

The Rules of Golf is an admirable book, containing some fine prose, and comparable in rhythm and directness to the Psalms of DAVID or other Hebrew poetry. Look up "wheelbarrow," for instance, in the index, and read aloud that noble passage:

"Any flag-stick, guide-flag, movable guide-post, wheelbarrow, tool, roller, grass-cutter, box, vehicle, or similar obstruction may be removed."

Note the majestic breadth of mind with which the word "similar" is used. And mark the simple lucidity of Rule 13:

"PLAYING A MOVING BALL

"A player shall not play while his ball is moving, under the penalty of the loss of the hole, except in the case of a teed ball, or a ball struck twice or a ball in water. When the ball only begins to move while the player is making his backward or forward swing he shall incur no penalty under this rule, but he is not exempted from the provisions of rule 12 (1) or rule 28 (1) and of rule 12 (3) and (4)."

Simpson can recite that rule. Not only can he recite it, but he knows what it means; and he can tell you its exact significance in all conceivable circumstances, with maps, instances, and illustrative anecdotes. That is the sort of man Simpson is.

Yet he is a God-fearing fellow, and no doubt we might have had a happy game; but it was June, and I am a victim of hay-fever. On the fourth green I sneezed. On the sixth green I sneezed. On the seventh green I sneezed five times. On the eighth green I suppressed a sneeze but giggled instead. At the ninth a cow mooed. At the tenth it mooed again. In every case, as Simpson pointed out, it cost him the hole.

"I wish you wouldn't sneeze on the green, old man," he said reproachfully, as if I had been saving the things up for the moment of his putt. Poor Simpson, he was three down, and he was rattled. And when he is rattled he falls back on the rules.

At the eleventh he played a wild approach shot. His ball bounded on to the green, rushed madly across it, and struck my bag of clubs which was lying at the edge of a young precipice just beyond.

"Ha!" said Simpson with quiet satisfaction, "my hole, I'm afraid."

"How's that?" said I innocently.

"It's the rule," said Simpson.

"But you haven't suffered. Your ball's still on the green. You'd be in that bunker now if you hadn't hit my bag. If I'd known you were going to bang the ball about in that fresh undisciplined fashion, I'd have buried my bag before you played. You deserve to lose *two* holes for a shot like that."

Simpson sighed wearily and began reciting. "If a player's ball when in motion," he intoned, "be interfered with in any way by an opponent, or his caddie, or his clubs, the opponent's side shall lose the hole. I'm sorry," he went on. "I hate winning a hole like that, but a rule's a rule, you know."

"Oh, very well," I said dignified-like. But on the next green I took careful aim with my putter and scored a direct hit on Simpson's bag at about thirty yards' range.

"Damned sorry," I said; "that's my hole, I fear."

"Here – you did that on purpose!" yelled Simpson.

"Oh, well, if we're playing bags, we're playing bags; and that's that," said I firmly, marching away to the next tee.

Relations were fairly strained for the rest of the game. I attempted no more bag shots, but Simpson held his clubs high in the air whenever I was putting.

At the last hole he was one up, but on the green I looked like squaring the match. Just before I made my crucial putt I observed a small object lying between my ball and the hole, and I stooped down, picked it up, and was about to throw it aside.

"Hi!" cried Simpson, "you can't do that. *That's a worm-cast.*"

"What of it?" said I.

"Why, you're not allowed to chuck it away like that. You must scrape it aside with a club. Look at your rules, man."

"Very well," I said, and, pulling out my little book of Rules, I turned to the invaluable index. "Dung... Etiquette... Water... Worm-casts...here we are."

I turned to page 17, and I read aloud the noble passage embodying that wondrous concatenation of diverse objects:

"Dung, worm-casts, snow, and ice may be scraped aside with a club..."

"There you are!" I cried in triumph. " '*May*,' not '*must*.' Why don't you study the rules, man?"

Simpson looked very angry.

"My good fellow," he said sternly, "I've played this game for twenty-five years, and what I don't know about it isn't worth knowing. The rule's perfectly plain. If there's a match, or a feather, or a stone on the green you can pick it up and throw it away. But if it's a worm-cast or a lump of ice you've got to scrape it away with a club."

"You're wrong," I said. "Anyhow, this isn't a worm-cast."

"What is it, then?" said Simpson, thoroughly worked up.

"It's a mole-hill," I said.

"You're a liar!" said Simpson.

"You're no gentleman," said I.

By this time there were about five couples standing about at various stages of the eighteenth hole, furiously waiting. In front of the club-house a small crowd was collected, watching our gentlemanly gesticulations. Out comes Matthews, a noted expert but a sensible fellow, and no friend of Simpson's.

"Time you fellows were moving on," he said. "What's the trouble?"

"Look at this," I said. "Simpson says it's dung, worm-casts, snow, or ice. I say it's a mole-hill. What do *you* think?"

Matthews gravely examined the object.

"You're both wrong," he said at last. "It's an ant-hill. Quite a small one, of course. An ant-hillock – strictly."

"Good Lord!" I said. "What's the rule about that?"

"Well, I don't know that the point has ever been decided. I expect we'll have to get a ruling on it. Will you come in, both of you, and see the Captain?"

"I know exactly what the rule is, thank you," said Simpson coldly. "Where *is* the Captain?"

"As a matter of fact he's in the bar."

"Oh, well," said Simpson, picking up his clubs.

"Oh, very well," said I.

4

WINTHROP

To be more accurate, Budd and Winthrop are People Nobody Plays Golf With Ever, for they are members of that notorious class of loafer, the Club-house Golfer, and he is a stout fellow who can drag them round the course even once.

And yet one should not laugh at them, for, poor devils they have the cruellest luck. Whenever Budd and Winthrop come down to the club it rains or, rather, whenever Budd and Winthrop come down to the club-house it is raining. People call them the Club Barometers. And if they have the luck to strike a fine day ten to one Budd has strained his shoulder, and Winthrop has just a touch of sciatica, and both of them are mere cripples as far as golf is concerned.

"Rough luck, old fellow," says everyone.

"Rough luck it is," says Budd, looking out wistfully to the first tee.

"Well, there's nothing for it but bridge, I suppose," sighs Winthrop.

"No use grumbling," says Budd bravely. "Good-bye, old chap; play well – wish I was coming with you. What's yours, Winthrop?"

"Mine's a gin-and-bitters, old boy."

And there we shall find them, patient, uncomplaining, when we come back from our round. Perhaps they have been able to get a bridge four together, or maybe potter about the billiard table with the help of a stick and a gin or two; or perhaps they have just snatched a little sleep in the reading-room. Anyhow, they don't go moaning about, cursing their luck, though you can see that they are fretting their souls out inwardly, longing to be away in the free fresh air.

No, they just keep a stiff upper lip and make pleasant conversation. For naturally, if there is any scandal going about, these two fellows have the pick of it. If there is one man who knows the whole truth about the Mrs Loam's dog episode, and can tell you the precise terms in which Mrs Loam insulted the secretary, it is Budd. And if there is a man living who can tell you the exact words in which the secretary made his infamous attack on Mrs Loam it is Winthrop.

Each of them has a man at bay in a corner now, and you can hear fragments of the whole truth leaking across the room from two sides.

"What exactly happened was *this*," says Budd in a confidential bellow. "The dog…the secretary…the dog… Then this woman said… What *he* said… Then that mangy hound… "

"Budd knows nothing about it," whispers Winthrop like a foghorn. "What happened was *this*… Miss Wriggle told me, and she was *there*. The dog… What's that?… Well, if you insist… Thanks, a gin-and-bitters… It's a nice dog, and she's a nice woman… A widow, yes… But old Fiddle-flick said. Damned rude, I call it… And all she said was… Meanwhile the dog… "

After that, if we behave nicely, Budd will get out his bag of clubs and tell us about them. For Budd has belonged to many golf clubs in his time, and, though no man can remember when he actually played a full round here, we know that in the past he has played many strange and glorious matches.

You can tell that from the number of clubs he possesses – such forests of drivers and brassies, such an armoury of irons and niblicks and mashie-niblicks, besides all sorts of weird unnatural hybrids at which the imagination boggles – gweeks, sniggers, and drafties, driving-niblicks, and putting-mashies (most of them illegal), and one hideous aluminium instrument with a twisted shaft which he calls a baffoon.

"With that putter," says Budd, fondling it affectionately, "I holed the winning putt in the Boxburgh Championship. This driver – ah!" and, rising shakily to his feet, he makes a few sentimental swings with it. "With this driver I carried the Precipice at Alpville in a snowstorm in 1910. Lord Bilberry gave me that cleek. That baffoon – did I ever tell you how I got that baffoon?"

No one speaks. We wait with breathless interest. For Budd has never yet acquired that club twice in the same way. One day we fear that his imagination will give out and we shall go back to the old story of the curate who drowned himself in a water-hazard after Budd had beaten him 10 and 8, and left Budd the club in his will.

"KING EDWARD VII gave me that club when he was Prince of Wales," says Budd, "in exchange for a cigar. We were playing at Yokohama," he adds, to make things quite clear.

We breathe again.

Winthrop, I admit, is often discovered strolling about outside the club-house with a putter or a mashie in his hand. No doubt you have seen those young men in riding-breeches who perambulate the streets of Oxford or Cambridge, slapping their gaiters with a whip, and obviously proceeding to or from a horse, though they are never actually detected on a horse. But Winthrop is not as they. For often, if the weather and the sciatica are not too bad, he does a little quiet putting-practice with a dozen balls or so on the second green, which is just under the lee of the bar. People keep playing the hole, of course, and then he has to stop putting and push his dozen balls away, which is vexing; but he looks a fine figure of a golfer as he stands there leaning on his putter in his balloon-like breeches, smoking his Dormie pipe.

"Not playing today, Winthrop?" one says.

"No, not today, old fellow," he says sadly. But one feels that it won't be *his* fault if he doesn't play tomorrow.

And once I actually began a round with Budd. What a scene it was! What a reckless buying of balls; what careful study of the weather forecasts; what eyeing of the cloudy skies! Budd was anxious, and Budd is a superb weather prophet. A great cheer went up from the members as Budd stepped off the first tee on to the Long Trail. I won the second hole, and was one up and sixteen to play. Budd felt a little faint, and had to drop into the club-house for a small restorative. At the fifth a hired man met him by arrangement with a gin and ginger beer. I was now three up. At the eighth it was tea-time, and we stopped and had a hearty meal at the Farm. Budd played the next hole gallantly in twelve. The next was the Mountain Hole, and Budd took a good pull at his flask. Then he took a good look at the sky.

"Rain!" he said, with a fearful oath. "Just my luck!"

Sure enough a drizzle began. Great drops of moisture fell pitilessly on our exposed faces. "Let's run for it," said Budd. And run we did.

A groan of sympathy went up as we re-entered the club-house. Poor old Budd's usual luck. Robbed of his round again.

5

RICKWOOD

Which is the more maddening – The Man Who Lets On That He Is A Great Deal Better Than He Really Is – or The Man Who Is A Great Deal Better Than He Lets On? Golf, I think, is the only game which produces the former in large numbers, because golf alone allows you, with care, to keep up the same bluff for a lifetime.

Rickwood is one of these men. I, of course, am the other kind of fellow. I played Rickwood the first day I visited the Club, a shivering new member. The secretary saw us both hanging about, and kindly introduced us. I felt at once that he was a regular tiger at the game: his cap, his knickerbockers, the way in which he bought a new ball (a sure sign), revealed him as an expert; and I wondered a little why such a man had not got a match in the ordinary way. I know now.

"Afraid I shan't give you much of a game," I said nervously as we walked out.

"Oh, that's all right," he said kindly. "What's your handicap?"

"About eighteen," I confessed. "What – er – what – I mean, what's yours?"

A little cloud passed over his brow.

"They've just pulled me down two," he said bitterly. "Goodness knows why. I'm quite off it these days."

"That's rotten, isn't it?" I sympathised. "What did you say your – ?"

"I'd better give you four strokes," said he. "Can't manage more, I'm afraid – not as I'm playing now."

"Thanks," I said gratefully. I saw then that the chivalrous fellow wanted to keep his handicap dark, so as not to frighten me.

The simple daisy grows richly about the first tee, and before we started Rickwood took a good many practice swings at these flowers. I watched in horror. The swish – the power of it! In half a minute there was not a daisy to be seen. Then he walked right away and with one blow destroyed a dandelion – simply slashed off its head. I saw that I was up against it indeed.

"Look at that *sand*," he said at last, seizing a handful and strewing it about the tee. "*Dry as dust*. Might as well try to tee up your ball on *castor-sugar!*"

However, in spite of the castor-sugar he hit a nice straight one down the middle.

"Good shot," I murmured enviously.

"Oh, *no*," he groaned in an agony. "No length – no *length!* I don't know what's the matter with me. Stiff! It's awful." And while I shakingly prepared my mountainous tee I could hear him with gloomy mutterings busily destroying more dandelions in the background.

I too had bought a new ball, one of those jolly one-and-sixpenny *Blue Spot Bishops* – all white and clean. I hit it quite hard and straight, but it was about ten yards behind Rickwood's *Purple Emperor* and I felt that it was no good.

"I don't like these *short* courses," he remarked as we walked on. "This is nothing but a drive and a pitch all the way round, if you're on your game."

"Rotten, isn't it?" I said politely, with my eye on the incredibly distant flag. "Do you come here often?"

"I've been here every summer for ten years," he said. "It's a filthy place. The secretary doesn't know his job. The greens are vile. The committee – Good God, did you see that?" And he stopped and stared after a maiden of engaging aspect who had just played a delicate shot with her spoon on the second hole. The sight pleased me.

"Rather a good one," I said mildly.

"Exactly," he replied. "But do you know what handicap they've given that girl? They've given that girl a handicap of thirteen. *Thirteen!* Why, she ought to be nine. It's a scandal, that's what it is."

I said nothing, but smote at my ball, and, in sheer terror of the man, missed it altogether.

Later (a good deal later) Rickwood picked my ball out of the hole for me and fingered it curiously.

"Are you playing with a *Bishop*?" he asked; and if he had said, "Are you playing with a weasel?" I could hardly have felt more profoundly ashamed.

"Aren't they any good?" I said humbly.

"They're all right for inland courses, I believe," said Rickwood, "but... Well, that's one up."

I hastily concealed my dear little *Bishop*, and hoped that my repainted *Major* was a more maritime ball.

On the second tee Rickwood pulled out his handkerchief and, holding it aloft, anxiously gauged the direction of the wind, which in my slipshod fashion I judged to be blowing in our faces.

"Against us," he announced at last. "We want a low one here."

He got it. It never rose an inch.

However, such was my respect for the man's powers that he won that hole, and the next, with consummate ease. The fourth we halved, for Rickwood had the bad luck to drive out of bounds into the road; and suddenly at the fifth I found that I was winning it, and winning it easily. When I was four (and "dead") and he was six (and some yards from the pin), he picked up his ball.

"It's no good," he said with resignation. "You get a stroke here."

"Oh," I said gratefully.

On the sixth tee he produced from his pocket what looked to me like a piece of green billiard chalk and carefully chalked the face of his driver. I watched with awe.

"A tip I got from ABE MITCHELL," he explained, though he did not explain the purpose of the rite. But I have always felt that billiards and golf have much in common.

Thereupon he struck his ball with the heel of his club into a small pot-bunker which belongs to another hole.

"Bad luck," I murmured. "What they call a losing hazard, isn't it?"

Happily Rickwood did not hear that silly impertinence. He was gazing ruefully at his hands.

"Blisters," he muttered. "Can't get a *grip*." It turned out that his blisters had been troubling him ever since we began, and I appreciated the good feeling that had kept him silent about them. And, in the circumstances, I did feel rather a pig about winning the next three holes.

At the tenth I was two up. I took my driver and was short. Rickwood took his iron. "Good Lord!" he cried a little later, "what the deuce do they put a bunker there for? I've seen seven men trapped in that bunker in the last two days!"

"Perhaps that's what it's for," I suggested tentatively.

"I shan't come to this place again," he said, and swung his niblick high. A cloud of sand rolled away, revealing the ball *in statu quo ante*, and Rickwood with a spasm of pain crossing his face. "By Jove," he said, rubbing his back, "I must be careful. I strained a muscle at Sandwich last year."

He struck three more careful blows, with much the same result. Then he said, " You get a stroke here," and picked up his ball.

By the fourteenth his back was paining him pretty considerably, and he could hardly hold the club for his blisters;

but he struggled gamely on, though of course the match had become a mere farce.

"One thing's quite certain," he said at last with a brave smile, "I can't give you four strokes in *this* condition. You know," he went on kindly, "you'd be quite a useful player if you took it up seriously."

I won 4 and 3. But it was a joyless victory. It was bad luck to have my first game at the club spoiled in this way; but when I told old Baggage, the captain, about it he only said, "Yes, it's an odd thing. I've played this game for twenty years and I've never beaten a man in perfect health yet."

I hate cynics. But just then my eye caught a list of Alterations of Handicap on the noticeboard, and I read:

"J RICKWOOD
Reduced from – 20 – to – 18."

6

COLLINS

Perhaps we may call Collins the Stormy Petrel of the links. He is as it were a Scourge, an Avenging Sword, and the Terror of Evil-doers. And the curious thing is that, whenever he is about, a sort of madness seems to possess mankind. With one accord they begin to do evil. And then there is a row.

And the worst of it is that somehow he usually manages to involve those with him in his rows So it was a most unfortunate accident that flung him into a foursome with Barber against the Archdeacon and myself – all exceedingly mild men. Barber, I must admit, is rather a maddening kind of golfer, for he is interested in Nature – flowers and birds and all that sort of stuff. So he walks round a golf course just as if it were an ordinary piece of country, looking at things.

Now Collins likes to play very fast. Or rather he likes "going through" people. Or rather he likes coming in and complaining that he has been "kept back all the way round."

Two girls started immediately in front of us, both good players, and one of them the charming but free-spirited Miss Greville, to whose favour Barber was by no means indifferent.

"We shall have to go through these women, I expect," said Collins, fidgeting about the tee. Miss Greville was indeed wandering in the rough, prodding Mother Earth with a niblick.

"By Jove, what a day!" said Barber, looking blissfully out to sea. "Just look at the light on the water over there."

"The late Bishop of Exeter," began the Archdeacon placidly, "was very fond of scenery. He told me once – "

"Look here, we can't stand here all *day*!" burst out Collins. "You'd better shout 'Fore!' Barber."

"Oh, there's no hurry," said Barber.

"Well, if *you* won't I *will*," said Collins, and, placing his hands to his mouth, he made a throaty but truculent trumpeting noise, which sounded like the exclamation of disgust so popular in historical novels: "FAUGH!"

The maidens appeared not to hear. He trumpeted again: "FAUGH!"

At that moment Miss Greville found her ball. "Too bad," said Collins, baulked of his prey. "Go on, Barber. You can drive now."

"Better wait a bit, hadn't I?" said Barber timidly, with his eye on the precious form of Miss Greville.

"We've waited long enough," snapped Collins. "You won't reach 'em, anyhow."

"That's true," said Barber; "I never get over this bunker;" and, thinking to please the man, he drove.

Alas, how beautifully! The ball whizzed into the wind, soared, hovered, and fell heavily a few yards beyond Miss Greville.

"I'm awfully sorry," cried the unhappy Barber into the wind; "I never thought – " The girl turned and looked at us, not, I regret to say, in forgiveness, but quite otherwise.

"Serve 'em right," said Collins.

From that moment he seemed to be possessed by one desire – to catch up "those women" and ruthlessly "go through" them. Barber also at first was anxious to come up within apologising distance; and so the two of them pressed on at a terrific pace, the Archdeacon and I panting astern. Several times during the first few holes Barber began shouting an apology; but it is very difficult to apologise gracefully in a loud voice at long range, and the ladies never seemed to hear.

The fourth, fifth, and sixth holes ran parallel. While we were playing the fifth Barber walked off rapidly to the right towards the ladies, raised his cap, and began again, "I'm awfully sorry – " Just then a yell of rage boomed across the links: "Hi!"

Barber turned around, as did everyone else for half a mile around and saw Collins wildly waving his cap at the retreating back of a gentle old man playing the fourth. The man took no notice.

"I say, Sir! Hi! *You*, Sir! Hi! Hullo!" shouted Collins, beside himself. "YOU'VE PLAYED WITH MY BALL!" The old man slowly ambled away.

"I'm afraid my father's a little deaf, Mr Barber," said Miss Greville icily. "You'd better tell your friend." And she passed on.

There was an unpleasant scene with Mr Greville, and at the end of it the ladies were a long way ahead. However, at the ninth there they were again, poking about in the rough.

"Too bad," said Collins with satisfaction, "holding us up *the whole way round*." Then he waited patiently for about five seconds and trumpeted again: "FAUGH!"

The ladies looked round, like frightened deer.

"May we go on?" shouted Collins with ill-assumed politeness.

The ladies made no reply, but suddenly found their ball and went on themselves.

"Too bad," said Collins. "Your drive, Barber. Let's get past these women, for goodness' sake."

But Barber and the Archdeacon were absorbed in the contemplation of a simple wildflower by the brook.

"The Lesser Celandine," said Barber; "*Ranunculus Ficaria*."

"Ah! *Ficus* – a fig," chuckled the Archdeacon. "Do men gather figs of the Lesser Celandine, then? Ha! And what is this charming purple blossom?"

"Bloody Crane's-bill, I think," said Barber. "*Geranium sanguineum*. Or else it's Dove's-foot."

"*Will you go on?*" roared Collins in a frenzy of impatience "We're not at Kew," he added with scathing irony. And Barber went on.

By a strange chance the same thing happened again – two or three times. The ladies would get well away ahead of us; then one of them would lose a ball; and then, just as Collins was confidently preparing to trample over their bodies, they would find it again and gaily proceed as if nothing had happened. It was extraordinary.

Meanwhile the round had not been without incident. At the eleventh a family party was picnicking on the cliff, and Collins made them re-pack their hampers and walk quarter of a mile away before he would consent to play the hole. At the twelfth two schoolboys were harmlessly practising mashie shots, and Collins gave them a dreadful wigging, on the ground that they were under sixteen and had no *locus standi*.

At the fourteenth a motorcar was halted on the cliff-road, almost on "the line." Under the car was a man. Collins shouted at him for a long time without effect, drove furiously at the car, missed it by fifty yards, and then, approaching, said hotly, "Look here, Sir – do you realise this is a *golf course?*"

The man emerged with great deliberation, spat on his hands, rubbed them with an oily rag, and replied, "Yus."

"Then why the devil don't you take your beastly car away?"

" 'Cos my ignition's all to blazes," said the man. "That's one reason. An' if you want any more you've only got to come under 'ere an' 'ave a look." And with these words the insolent mechanic disappeared again. Collins took the number of his car.

By this time, for some obscure reason, I felt thoroughly ashamed of myself; and the Archdeacon looked as if he had just robbed a church.

At the seventeenth we came up with the two ladies again, sitting on the tee and gazing thoughtfully into space.

"Ha!" said Collins, "going to let us through. About time too. If you hadn't wasted so much time over that confounded flower at the ninth, Barber, we'd have gone through them ages ago."

Just then Miss Greville rose and leisurely teed her ball, remarking audibly to her companion, "Yes, I think that's the prettiest view on the whole course." As she walked off one at least of her beautiful eyes caught mine; and had I not known her to be a perfect lady I could have sworn that the expression in it amounted to a wink.

But, alas, a marriage has *not* been arranged between Miss Mary Greville and Mr Sidney Barber. And, as for the Archdeacon and myself, we entered the club-house with downcast eyes, feeling that we had alienated the affections of the entire human race.

"Extraordinary people you get down here," said Collins. "Don't seem to understand the *etiquette* of the game."

7

POSTSCRIPT

Perhaps you are bored by all this golf. Then take heart. For there *is* a way of escape, even from the golf-bore. Or, rather, there is a way of correction. But a man must have a straight face and a steely heart to take it. It is no good sitting down under the oppressor; if you do you are crushed. You must stand up and fight him.

John and George had been playing golf together and visited me in the evening. Unfortunately George arrived an hour after John, so that I had heard the authorised version of the round from John long before George began. But, happily, I had a confederate named Thompson there too. When George had reached the third hole (in the revised version) I said dreamily: "That reminds me; I had a rather curious experience today – "

"Up till then I was one under fours, but I topped my drive – " said George.

"I had a rather curious – "

"John was in the pig-sty," said George, "which is out of bounds. You know the one I mean?"

"I had a rather curious experience today," I went on blandly (if a host cannot be firm who *can* be?); "I think it might interest you."

"Um," said George, as politely as he could. "I happened to be at Covent Garden Station with Williams. You know it, don't you? It has yellow tiles, like jaundice."

"Yes – *rather*," said Thompson.

"Well, we wanted to get to Shepherd's Bush, and we wanted to get there by four o'clock."

"By Jove!" said Thompson.

George looked at him doubtfully, but murmured at last, "No – really?"

"We took our tickets in the ordinary way – at the ticket-office, you know. We went into the lift – that's one of the stations where they have lifts, you remember – and we went down in it. When the gates were opened I was standing absolutely clear of them, and practically not smoking at *all*. I'll swear to that – "

I paused here and blew a meditative cloud of smoke into the air, in the manner of the trained *raconteur*.

Thompson leaned forward eagerly. "Go on," he said.

"*I* walked out of the lift first – "

"Really?" said Thompson.

"No, not really. Now I come to think of it, Williams did. Anyhow we both left the lift quite safely, and walked down to the platform. Up to this point nothing had happened *at all*; you understand?"

"Yes," said George, rather grimly, I thought.

"Now the odd thing was this – the very first train that came in stopped at the station. Very often, you know, they have trains which don't stop at that station – simply go bang through without stopping. Non-stop trains, you know,"

"Yes," said John, with an expression of pain.

"Well, we got into the train; I forgot what sort of carriage it was, but it was either a smoker or one of those carriages where you can't smoke – you know the ones I mean? It must have been about half-past three then."

I paused again – as one getting the whole thing straight in his mind.

"The train started and we went through station after station. Williams had been playing golf, and he began to tell me a few things about his round. By Jove, the things that fellow told me about the seventh hole! Marvellous – *simply* marvellous!"

"Yes?" said John, brightening a little.

"Well, you know how that sort of story gets hold of you. And – this is an interesting thing – we ought, of course, to have changed at Piccadilly Circus, but I was so wrapped up in that fellow's seventh hole – he drove into the haystack and hooked his second into the sea, you know – "

"Yes, I know that haystack," said George happily. "One day last summer – "

"As I was saying, we were so wrapped up that *we never got out at Piccadilly at all!* The first thing we knew we were at Dover Street. What do you think of *that*?"

I leaned back in my chair and laughed till I cried. John and George looked as if they might cry too at any moment, but they smiled stiffly and made polite murmurs of stupefaction.

"Well, then things began to happen. We decided we would go on to Hammersmith and take a tram. At Down Street I stood up and gave my seat to a lady – simply stood up and held on to a strap. At Hyde Park – no, at Hyde Park we didn't stop – just dashed through. *It was a non-stop train.*"

"Good heavens!" said Thompson.

"At Knightsbridge a good many people got out and I sat down again. But just at the last moment a lady got in and Williams had to give her *his* seat. So I was sitting down and he was standing up. You follow? I suppose it was about twenty to four then. Where was I?"

"At Knightsbridge," said Thompson, blowing his nose. Thompson seemed to have a bad cold. As for John and George their eyes were like the eyes of a dead mackerel, fixed and filmy. Their faces were crystallised in that painful semi-smirk of ill-assumed interest and patient anticipation which one has felt so often on one's own face, but happily never seen. I knew then what I must have looked like as John approached the fifteenth hole. But I was ruthless.

"At Brompton Road – do you know Brompton Road Station, John?"

"What? No. I mean yes – yes."

John had gone to sleep; I could not allow that.

"Well, it doesn't matter, because nothing much happened *there*. But at South Kensington – you know South Kensington, George?"

"Oh, yes."

"I mean, do you know the *Station* – because it makes all the difference?"

"Yes, I know it."

"I mean the *Tube* Station, not the District?"

"*Yes*," said George, in the tone of a man about to scream.

"Well, it has black and blue tiles, and I know we stopped there, because of a rather curious coincidence.

I paused and lit my pipe; then I went on impressively, "*Those colours were the colours of my old house at school.*"

"Good *Lord!*" said Thompson, and had a violent coughing fit.

"By Jove, yes, that sort of thing makes a man think. But somehow or other we got away from that station, and the next thing – or the next but one – was that we were at Earl's Court. Now I want you to listen carefully to this – "

They listened carefully, as men hopefully scenting a climax afar off.

"Williams, you remember, was standing up, but at Earl's Court he sat down again. Oh, by the way, at Earl's Court there's a moving staircase. Do you know it, George?"

"Yes; but why did you go up *that*?"

"We didn't. I only mention it because I went up it one day last summer when I was playing – travelling with Thompson. Didn't we, Thompson?"

But Thompson was coughing very dangerously in the window.

"Well, at West Kensington we both stood up. So we were all square. At Baron's Court he stood up and I sat down. That made me dormy one. Halfway to Hammersmith he sat down on the floor and was disqualified. At Hammersmith we simply walked out of the train and took the tram to Shepherd's Bush. And, by Jove, we arrived there at *six minutes past four*."

There was a long, long silence.

"What exactly was the point of your story?" said John at last.

"Well, I thought you'd like to hear how I spent my day. But you haven't told us about the fourth hole, George."

"I think we'd better go," said John.

They never came back. But it is expedient that one man should lose his friends for the people.

MARINERS OF ENGLAND

BEING EXTRACTS FROM THE LENGTHY AND RATHER
TEDIOUS LOG OF THE "*CLIO*"

1

THE SHARK

"Can we get away tonight?" asked the owner of the *Clio* as we pushed the dinghy off.

"Ay," said old Joe of Needleport and spat regretfully into the harbour. "You'll have a nice tide under you from six o'clock. Fine weather comin' and a full moon."

Tonight! How thrilling! This very night we were to put out to sea and sail along the Channel of Old England under a full moon. What would the *Clio* be like? A "yacht," at any rate, we knew from her captain, though a mere nine tons, but of what shape, of what rig and, most important, of what colour? Never mind; tonight we should be away in her. Old Joe had been looking after her for seven months (at ten shillings a week), and for the last few weeks, we knew, had been busily engaged in making her ready for sea.

It is odd that those two noble things, the horse and the boat, should so corrupt the souls of men. In the United States I saw seventy-nine statues of GEORGE WASHINGTON. All except one wore the painfully virtuous expression of the canonical legends, but that one had a hard, no-nonsense, man-of-the-world aspect which was quite shocking. And the explanation, I heard, was simply this – that the sculptor had made his preliminary studies of the face while GEORGE WASHINGTON was in the act of selling a horse. Boats have the same effect. I would not trust an archbishop who was selling me a boat. Horse-copers and stable-boys, I understand, are rough, rapacious persons, but I wager they cannot hold a candle to the longshoreman. And I have known many of these simple, manly, weather-beaten sharks, but old Joe of Needleport is surely king of them all.

He rowed us slowly out to the *Clio* in the fading light, grey and bearded, tanned by the pitiless suns of Devon, and worn with a lifetime of rowing about the harbour of Needleport; and, as he rowed, the thought of the *Clio* and his labours upon her seemed to be more than he could bear.

"Many and many a sleepless night she's given me," he croaked, resting on his oars; and his watery old eyes wandered pathetically from face to face. "Turr'ble gales from the souwest… Boats carryin' away from their moorin's right and left… Many a night I've lain awake thinkin' of 'er… I wouldn't go through it again, not for no money, I wouldn't."

"Ah," said the Master of the *Clio*.

"Night after night. Lyin' awake in me bed…Wore me out, it 'as," said old Joe.

"Ah," replied the Master of the *Clio*; and old Joe began to row again, but feebly now, as if indeed his stamina was giving out.

"She be turr'ble old," he went on quaveringly. "Started leaking las' week she did," and a slow tear leaked in sympathy out of the corner of his right eye.

"How's that? She never leaked before," said the Captain.

"Tight as a drum she's been these seven months. Then las' week she let in fower inches of water, sudden like. Monday there were six inches. Never seed such a thing in my life. I been pumping 'er out twice a day. Wore me out, she 'as"; and once again he stopped rowing.

"Very odd she should spring a leak just before I want her," said the Captain.

"Likely there'd be a bit of oakum worked out of they seams," said old Joe, ignoring the oddity referred to. "Turr'ble warm suns there's been 'ere," he added.

"Ah," said the Captain, who had not seen the sun for six weeks.

"Pumped 'er out this marnin', I did," said Joe. "She be dry as I be now. Many a sleepless night – " he went on, but caught somebody's eye and stopped.

We boarded the *Clio* in silence and peered down the hatchway into the tiny cabin, as men look down into a disused well. The cabin was full of damp vapour. Where the cabin floor should have been there was a sheet of water, green and noisome, like the water of a stagnant pond, the water of ages, gently slushing to and fro as the boat rolled. Water-beetles swam happily upon the surface. Underneath one felt that there were fish.

"Never seed such a thing," said old Joe, astonished. "Pumped 'er out this marnin', I did."

"Ah," said the Captain. "What about the rigging?"

"Runnin' riggin' be turr'ble rotten," said old Joe. "Look at *that*, now," and, seizing one of the more important ropes, he tugged at it smartly with both hands. The rope came in two.

"And look at *that*!" the old man cried with growing enthusiasm, hauling madly on the peak-halyard. The halyard broke in three places.

"And do 'ee look at *this*," he said, tearing one of the stays from its place. "And this – and this!" Two heavy things called blocks fell upon our heads. The man was warming to his work. Dejectedly we clambered round the boat, watching old Joe breaking her up. When he had done she looked like the refuse of a shipchandler's establishment.

"Decks leak," said the weather-beaten old shark cheerfully, plunging a huge knife into one of the seams. A stream of rainwater trickled on to the cabin seats.

"I wouldn't go to sea in this yacht, not for no money, I wouldn't," he croaked again. "Your mains'l's turr'ble rotten."

"But it oughtn't to be *here*," protested the Captain. "You ought to have kept it under cover *ashore*."

"Las' wek I 'ad 'er out and dried 'er. Pretty nigh every week I've dried that sail," quavered the old man, removing the cover. The cover was green with *algae*. From underneath it two birds emerged, and flew away, flapping their wings. The nest was perfectly formed.

Then at last the Captain uplifted his voice. He is a man of letters, and he spoke winged words.

"Old Joe," he said, "you aged liar, you simple, shameless, incompetent liar, for seven months you have left this noble ship to rot upon the waters; you have made her within as a large Aquarium, and without as a small Zoo. You say truly that she is rotten, and you have made her rotten. For this service you do confidently expect to receive the sum of fifteen pounds. No such sum shall be granted unto you. Liar, thief, despoiler of mariners, cursed be your name and the name of all longshoremen, but especially the longshoremen of this iniquitous port! May never a ship or boat put into this place for shelter! May it be marked upon the Admiralty Chart as a wicked place, a danger to the sailor and the home of robbers; that thus the longshoremen of Needleport may perish utterly from the face of the earth! God Save the King!

"And now begone from me, lest I do you a mischief; but take with you the sum of five pounds, that haply in the 'Sailor's Arms' you may drink a little of the filthy beer of Needleport, and die."

Old Joe climbed into his dinghy and got out his oars.

"I've been shipmates with the likes of you," he observed darkly. "You wouldn't believe the trouble I've 'ad with that boat."

"I wouldn't," said the Captain.

Then the old man rowed away into the dusk, and over the still water there came for a time the sound of his indignant mumbles: "Many and many a sleepless night... Wore me out, she 'as...lyin' awake..."

Silence fell at last and the night came down upon us.

"Well, we shall have to spend the night *here*, that's all," we said cheerfully "But first let's go ashore and be merry at an inn."

Then we discovered a new thing. The dinghy of the *Clio* was missing. We were cut off from Needleport, alone and friendless in a porous boat.

"Old Joe," we cried into the darkness, "come back, come back! Nice old Joe, come back to us."

But answer came there none.

Then it began to rain.

2

THE WRECKERS

"*Keep close to the coast and have courage,*" said the French Admiral in the twelfth and last paragraph of his Sailing Instructions to the West African convoy. And that has been our working motto. It is indeed a wise and pleasant thing to have the land, however rocky, within reasonable swimming distance. And on a stormy night the Mariner does well to keep the lights of Bournemouth in sight, reminding him that after all there are worse places than the sea.

But not many. And looking through the Log of this tremendous voyage on the high seas, I see that the really great moments were those we spent upon the land recuperating. What goodly and joyful places are the Saloon Bars of the Harbour Inns at —, —, —, —, and —! Do not misunderstand me. There are yachtsmen, I know, who are content to dine and sleep upon their yachts in carefully selected havens, joining it by train at the next port; but we are not of those. All our sailing has been done by sea. I merely remark – How goodly and joyful it is to arrive at the places mentioned on the South Coast!

And this is odd, when you consider how thick upon that coast is the generation of evil men. Few, indeed, are the innkeepers like Mr Treasure of the "Greyhound" at —, a man of such benignity and tact that it was as much as we could do to make him present us with a bill. Food, wine, and dry clothes were heaped upon us, and, if he could in any way contrive it, *gratis*. All other hotel-keepers have invariably made us pay for everything we had — the low skunks.

Then there was the simple, unspoiled community of —. Late one night, sailing like an angel in the cloudy moonlight, the *Clio* came swiftly into a place called Dead Man's Cove, a place of steep beaches and high forbidding cliffs, a small edition of Gibraltar, but without the harbour. It stands wide open to the southwest, and if the wind blows from that quarter, a huge sea comes out of the Atlantic, and, snatching up the Mariner's ridiculous boat, batters it to fragments on the toughest kind of rock.

"In 1823," says the little book cheerfully, "in a westerly gale, three transports were smashed to pieces in Dead Man's Cove, with great loss of life."

But tonight the wind was easterly, and we were very wet. The *Clio* headed gaily for the dusky shore. Peter and I stood in the bows, gingerly preparing the intolerable anchor.

Out of the darkness came a gruff but helpful voice:

"Boat ahoy! You can't anchor here."

"Can't I!" said Peter, and let the vile thing go.

After that, as is the custom of the sea, we rapidly rowed ashore. Suddenly out of nowhere appeared some thirty shadowy figures. Ah! the rough good-hearted fishermen, how they ran down the beach to meet us, and with glad cries hauled the dinghy up the precipitous beach, with many a "Ha!" and "Ho!" and also "Up she comes!"

"Cheerily, my lads!" I cried, bending my body with a will, but taking care not to strain myself.

Yes, they were glad to see us, those fisherfolk. We loaded them with thanks. They would not accept them. What *did* they want? we wondered. Ah!

It was years, one gathered, since any Mariner had been fool enough to anchor in that place, and all their minds were full of that occasion. One veteran, with the splendid *camaraderie* of the sea, proceeded to predict every kind of misfortune for the *Clio*. The others crowded behind him, muttering grimly in the moonlight, like the Chorus of a Greek play; and every now and then the word "Redwing" came to our ears, and always with the hint of doom.

"This be a terrible bad place to lie," said the veteran proudly.

"Ay, 'tes a wicked place," said another, with gusto. "Happen the wind goes westerly, she'll be on they rocks in no time."

"Ay," boomed the Chorus gleefully, "she will so."

"What weight anchor have you?" asked the Chorus Leader.

"About a ton," said I, having had some dealings with the thing.

"That won't hold her, nor two tons neither," was the sorrowful reply. "Terrible bad holding that be. Now if that was my boat d'you know what I'd do?"

"No," said our Captain politely.

"I'll tell you what I'd do if that was my boat. I'd put three or four young fishermen aboard, so's they'd be handy if the wind went west. D'ye see that moon?" he added with sudden intensity, gripping the Captain's shoulder.

"I see it," said the Captain. The moon looked normal.

"Westerly wind, for sure," said the wise old liar.

"Ay, 'tis a westerly moon," boomed the Chorus.

"Well, I'll risk it," said the Captain; "the fact is, I wouldn't ask any of you to spend a night in that boat. She's not fit for human consumption. You'd get your feet wet. She leaks."

"Is that so?" said one hopefully. "Maybe she'd want pumping out during the night?"

"Happen she'd sink before morning," said another.

"I wouldn't like to see her sink where she's lying now," said the leader. " 'Tis a wicked place for a boat to sink. Terrible deep watter that be. Fifty fathom, or more."

"Sixty," corrected another.

"More like seventy," said a fifth. "D'ye mind the *Redwing*?"

"Ay, the *Redwing*," said every man darkly.

"Well, I'll risk it," said the Captain again. "Where's the nearest hotel?"

In the pale light an expression of infinite reproach was visible on all those weather-beaten faces. It was almost more than we could bear. But we bore it. We went away to bed.

Next morning when we leapt from our beds about noon, the wind was still safely northeast, and the *Clio* still rolled bonnily in the August rain. Circumstances prevented us from sailing that day. All day it rained, and we chafed in the billiard-room, sighing for the open sea. And all day the thirty fisherman leaned gloomily against "The Crab and Mackerel," staring the lonely *Clio* out of countenance. When we returned from pumping her out, willing hands did not haul the dinghy up the beach. But one of the honest fellows observed:

"I wouldn't leave that boat with no one in 'er tonight, I wouldn't, not if she was mine. Wind's going westerly."

"Not tonight," I said, knowingly. "Do you see that cloud?"

"Ay."

"That's a sure sign," I said. "Besides, it's Monday."

The man looked at me with a new respect, as one sailor looks at another.

Next morning, sure enough, the wind was south-west, light but freshening. The *Clio* had already dragged her anchor and was appreciably nearer the rocks. Just before going on board to get up sail we happened to enter the inn – to replenish our water-jars. All the fishermen were there, all discussing the *Clio*, but now, it seemed, with a new hopefulness. A bright fire burned in the grate, and, after all, there is nothing like the cheerful fires of August.

"Good day, Captain," cried the veteran. "What be you hurryin' away for? Bide along here another night and go away with the marnin' tide, Captain."

"Ay, 'tis a fine little harbour, so it is," said another. "You've no need to sail today, Captain."

"Wind's getting up," said we. "She's dragged a long way already."

"Not she – she's never moved an inch," they cried. "Wind's droppin', Captain. Don't you leave us, Captain."

Loyal fellows – they had learned to love us. We gave them beer. But as we parted I said to one of them:

"Do you mind telling me about the *Redwing*?"

"Ah!" he answered with a friendly wink. "Why, Sir, she ran on they rocks las' September and kep' us all in firewood ever since. We be terrible short now. We thought maybe you'd help us out like." And he looked with melancholy at the dying fire.

"Well, you'll never burn *our* boat," I told him. "She's much too wet."

"You never know," he said kindly. "Goodbye, Sir – and come again."

3

THE LOBSTER

About 9.0 a.m., we made the port of Ryde. For six hours of darkness we had battled with a raging wind. We had struggled past *The Shambles*. We could have thrown a stone on to *The Shingles*. We tossed biscuits on to *The Brambles*. We had travelled fifty-five miles. We were wet through. Sleepless and unshaven, we approached the Isle of Wight as men who have been through a great naval engagement, conscious of our worth. Surely the whole town would leap from their beds to shout a welcome to the storm-tossed Mariners!

But we had forgotten. It was Ryde Week. Scrubby and bedraggled, the *Clio* crept to her anchorage among the pure white yachts of princes, peers, and titled grocers, with the sensations, I imagine, of a black sheep entering for the first time a flock of white ones. It was a stirring spectacle. The White-Winged Doves of the Solent, as the picture-papers call them, had not yet spread their wings. Their owners were still trying to snatch a wink of sleep ashore. But the morning toilet had begun. On every snowy deck two or three able-bodied valets in blue jerseys were already at work, busy at the immemorial duties of the sea. To every man a tin of brass-polish, to every man a duster or two. How they rubbed, the sturdy fellows! Here a little, there a little – rub, rub, rub! Here, one felt, the spirit of NELSON, of DRAKE, and FROBISHER breathed again. And what looks of proper scorn they flung upon the *Clio!* Many of the Doves were already gay with signal-flags, and one felt that each was making the same terrific signal: "NO BOATS ALLOWED HERE EXCEPT IN EVENING DRESS."

Naturally we were too ashamed to stay on board. Better to breakfast ashore than face the due contempt of all those able-bodied housemaids. We went ashore.

At the pier an aged shark shooed us away. We had forgotten to varnish the dinghy.

"You can't bring that there boat in 'ere," he shouted malignantly. "She'll be in the way of they motor-boats."

"Good," we said, and tied her up at both ends.

In the hall of the — Hotel we met some real sailors about to breakfast, magnificent men in white ducks and yachting-caps, and wearing that freshly-boiled-lobster complexion which only the very wealthiest sailors attain. Slinking under their lee we interviewed the headwaiter. The head-waiter had an eloquent eye.

We said in an off-hand manner, "We have been sailing all night. We have weathered a quite exceptional storm. *The Shambles, The Shingles, The Brambles* – all these obstacles sought to destroy us. We baffled them. We are tired. Can we have some bacon and eggs?"

Did the eye of the headwaiter reply, "Gentlemen, thank Heaven you are safe. You are now in the holy haven of the amateur sailor. You have done well. You are welcome"? It did not.

It said, "Go forth out of this, you odious penniless creatures, lest the mere sight of your disgusting grey-flannel trousers contaminates the breakfast of a single lobster-face."

But, thank Heaven, this is a free country. After a good deal of palaver we were served with breakfast in the coffee-room – behind a screen.

Lounging afterwards in the lounge, which seemed to be rolling, pitching, and heaving generally in a very curious way, we were searchingly examined by an exceptionally fine lobster, evidently the King Lobster of the entire herd. A telescope was under his arm. A little compass dangled on his watch-chain. M.Y. *Bogus* was printed largely on his yachting cap. I saw at once that he was a man of the very highest birth. After a little the manageress appeared and joined in the scrutiny. We felt as the earwig feels when someone suddenly removes his brick.

"Will I lend the gintleman my field-glasses?" said Peter loudly, breaking into the best Irish. "Sure he can't make us out, is it centipedes we are or what."

"Faith, and why wouldn't he use the fine telescope he has on him?" said I.

"It could be that it doesn't open at all," said Peter, trying not to giggle. "For I've seen prettier telescopes in the big toy shops that do be in Dublin and Killarney and Innisfree itself."

"It might," said I, drying up lamentably.

"It's a quare hard thing, so it is," says Peter, with a fierce expression, "for three poor paytriots to be looked at in that way in the early mornin' before the dew is off the bog, and they destroyed travellin' on the great sea. Will I show him the little gun I have in me pocket, the craythur?"

"You will not then," I said, "for it's scarce he's made himself."

Indeed, by this time the King Lobster had fled. The manageress had bolted into her office, no doubt to telephone the police. Quickly, but with dignity, we evacuated the Hotel and rowed out to the *Clio*.

Getting under way we passed under the stern of a large white motor yacht – curiously enough the M.Y. *Bogus*. Pure White Dove! Her silver cigar-box shone in the sun. Her deckchairs stood in trim rows, ready for sea. From her stern there issued the jolly sea-smell of petrol and boiled cabbage. We bade the goodly ship and all that goodly company of grocers an austere farewell.

"Farewell," we cried. "Sea-hogs! Snobs! Lobsters, and the sons of lobsters, farewell! Cursèd be they who go down to the sea in motor-yachts, and cling like shell-fish to the Isle of Wight! For these are they who have made the noble sport of yachting to stink in the nostrils as the sport of lobsters. Farewell! we pass to a purer sea, where there are neither motors, nor fumes of motors, nor fat white men with nursery telescopes. Farewell, and follow not!"

It is doubtful if the crew of the *Bogus* understood sufficient of this address to report to their Captain, but they gave the cigar-box another rub and waved their dusters at us in a friendly way.

That evening we stood on the mainland in the garden of Mr Splick, who makes a "specialty" of Lobster Teas. Mr Splick has two enormous seawater tanks, peopled only by thousands of live lobsters. We watched them for a long time, some clinging motionless to the side, some crawling round and round their spurious sea, but all slowly fattening for the hour of death – a hideous spectacle.

The sun went down and darkness fell upon the lobsters. John made an eloquent gesture towards the more westerly pond.

"Cowes," he said briefly.

"Ryde," said I, from the bank of the other one.

Next evening our Captain had left us, and at about 4 p.m. we were bowling merrily down Southampton Water. The sun was shining, and by clever manoeuvring we had extracted two hoots from that giant liner the *Neurasthenia*, costing the company I don't know what. We were very gay.

At about 4.10 I steered the *Clio* at a brisk pace on to the Hamble Spit.

"Scandalise the mains'l," said I, knowing exactly what to do.

"Right," said Peter, and he did it.

At 9.30 p.m. we were still scandalising the mainsail on the Hamble Spit when out of the gloom a thick voice hailed us: "Can we give you a tow off?"

"You can," we said gratefully. And towed off, with difficulty, we were.

But, alas, the voice was the voice of the King Lobster, and we anchored that night under the stern of the good ship *Bogus*.

It is a hard life, the sea.

ETCETERA

A "RAG"

In the town of Coxburgh there dwelt a man, whose name I do not know; but his name, like the rest of him, was of no importance. Let him answer to "Hi," like the gentleman in *The Snark*. Now this Hi had no money and no work; in fact he was a thoroughly low fellow. And one day his sense of the unfitness of things so worked upon his mind that he rose up in a public place and made a speech about it.

In the course of his address he uttered certain opinions of a revolutionary nature, but mildly enough, for he was a mild little man; so mild that no one in the audience treated his remarks with any seriousness. In fact they laughed. Nor would the police have taken him seriously if he had not chosen to deliver his address in a place in which it was not customary to deliver revolutionary addresses. He delivered it in an open space off the public highway where the statue of a benevolent mayor had been erected; and this space was so small that the audience which gathered to laugh at the ridiculous little man overflowed on to the public highway and obstructed the traffic, seriously delaying the progress of a municipal tram.

Now in this country, quite rightly, it is one thing to preach revolution in a mild way, but it is quite another thing to obstruct a municipal tram. Mr Hi was arrested. In the course of the police-court proceedings it came out that he had been preaching revolution; and though the fair-minded constable added that his audience had treated him as a joke the magistrate remarked, very properly, that in these times revolution was no joke, and no man must speak lightly of it, especially if in so doing he hindered his fellow-citizens in the exercise of their common liberties. And he was compelled to treat Mr Hi a little more seriously than Mr Hi's audience had treated him. Mr Hi raised no objection, for he was a mild man and knew that he had done wrong.

Now in this town there was a University for the sons of gentlemen. And in it there was one whom we will call ffoulkes FitzEustace, for want of a worse name. And one day, as he sat in the barber's shop, idly turning over an old local paper, his eye caught the account of Mr Hi's trial. It caught the words "revolution" and "joke," and in his fertile brain there sprang and burgeoned an idea. The end of his last term was but a few days distant and time hung heavy on his hands; for FitzEustace was not "seeking honours," and honours of no kind had been thrust upon him.

But at least he could "go down" in a blaze of glory. And he conceived with rapture the majestic notion of a Mock Revolution.

So it came to pass that when Mr Hi emerged from the common prison, chastened and repentant, but not less low than before, he beheld in the public streets a strange thing. A large body of high-spirited young gentlemen were marching in procession, headed by FitzEustace and a mock Soviet, in false black beards and extraordinary costumes. They carried banners, on which were blazoned, but, of course, in fun, sentiments of the most appallingly subversive character. They also carried mock revolvers with cardboard barrels, which they flourished at the spectators as they passed; and these weapons in the most laughable fashion squirted a stream of water into the faces of the citizens.

Some of the students had mock knouts, and even mock bombs composed largely of decaying cabbage, and these, when flung among the crowd with mock ferocity, caused intense amusement. None laughed so heartily as Mr Hi, who received the full force of an unusually decayed bomb in his face.

Thus the light-hearted young gentlemen marched in triumph round the town. A few policemen had early attached themselves to the procession, but, seeing the fun of the thing and indeed being powerless to do anything else, contented themselves with marching in front, in order to see that the procession was not obstructed. For this, of course, would have obstructed the traffic. Readily enough the carts and motor-cars drew into the kerb and halted to let the jolly boys go by. And how the owners of the cars laughed as one after another the students blew their horns for them or playfully banged them on the head with bladders! It was a gay scene.

Mr Hi followed with large numbers of the mere townsfolk; and at length the Soviet reached the little space where he had made his famous speech. And here, for he was by now tired of walking, the gay and ingenious FitzEustace decided that he would hold an Extraordinary Commission for the Punishment of Counter-Revolutionaries. Mounting the steps of the late mayor, whose person they decorated with stray fragments of cabbage and old newspapers, the Soviet proceeded to try, and condemn to hideous deaths, a number of undergraduates suspected of reactionary tendencies.

This was extremely entertaining, and a vast and hilarious crowd filled the street, through which the police with difficulty forced a passage for the municipal trams. All other vehicles were diverted to a different route, that none of the merry-makers might be injured.

Thus all went well; but at last, ever ready for fresh diversions, FitzEustace beheld one of the municipal trams, half-full of citizens and inextricably bogged in the crowd before him; and it became clear to him that the tram was a nest of counter-revolutionaries. At his command the fearless youths, in the most gentlemanly manner conceivable, boarded the tram and proceeded to eject the occupants. It was through a pure misunderstanding that the conductor's roll of tickets was distributed among the crowd, and it was by the merest accident that the hat of the conductor was transferred to the head of the late mayor. The conductor was a good fellow and saw the joke immediately.

But now it seemed to the police that the joke, though side-splitting, had continued long enough; so they ejected the students from the tram and desired FitzEustace to desist from his operations. To this he replied with witty prevarications, after which a constable gently but firmly laid a hand upon his shoulder, suggesting at the same time that he should descend from his post of vantage. FitzEustace then uttered a valiant cry of "Comrades! to the rescue!" Thereupon a great number of chivalrous youths, and not a few of the mere townsfolk, rushed to his rescue. Among these last was the mild-mannered Mr Hi. He had no particular love for FitzEustace, but he was a romantic, and he had reasons for believing that policemen were generally in the wrong.

At this moment there was a cry from one of the undergraduates, announcing the approach of the Proctors, or those responsible for the discipline of the young gentlemen. And at that cry the audacious boys rapidly withdrew in all directions.

Thus the Proctors on their arrival found a harassed constable, holding in one hand the gay and generous FitzEustace, and in the other the unspeakable Hi, who had been immediately recognized and seized as a rowdy already known to the police.

FitzEustace was delivered over to the Proctors for disciplinary treatment by the University authorities. He was, of course, "sent down" with ignominy, thus losing the last three days of his last term. But he went down, like the sun, in a blaze of glory.

And Mr Hi, in the common prison, pondered deeply the mysteries of life.

PIN-DROPS

The Scene is a stand at Lord's Cricket Ground. The Time is about half-way through one of the most important matches of the season. Anyone who reads his paper properly would learn that at this period it was possible to hear a pin drop anywhere in the vast ground. Anyone, however, who was actually present in this stand would easily have failed to hear the dropping of a barrelful of crowbars. What he did hear was an immense babble consisting of fragments such as these:

An Enthusiast (darkly). FOUR byes.
2nd Enthusiast (controversially). No, he hit it.
1st Enthusiast (firmly). Leg-byes.
A Lady. What I say is, a girl of her age can't know her own mind, and it's no good saying she can. Where are you lunching?
2nd Lady (who flatters herself that she is an enthusiast too). Oh, do be quiet Betty. Well *hit*, Sir! There's Major Grange! He hasn't seen us. Who's that with him? What a pretty girl!
Betty. Shockingly dressed (*Raising her voice*) Major Grange! Wave to him, Maud. (*Standing up*) Major Grange! (*Shouting*) Major Grange!

[*A wicket falls*]

Maud (annoyed). There, they've put him out, and I never saw. Why can't you be quiet, Betty? *Major Grange!*

The Man About Town

A Young Man (*to some American citizens under his wing*). Well, what do you think of it?

1st American (*cautiously*). Sir, your national game is a vurry remarkable institootion. (*To his daughter*) Say, Mamie, Mr Roberts here would be glad to know your reactions to the British national game.

Mamie (*brightly*) Why, I'm just tickled to death, Poppa. Guess it's as lively as Madam Toosso's on a Sunday morning – isn't it, Champ?

Champ (*gloomily*). It sure is.

Poppa (*courteously*). Mr Roberts, Sir, I'd be glad to have you instruct me in the principles of this game. Seems to me I have the background pretty clear in my mind, but figgering out the details is a vurry different proposition.

Mr Roberts (*nobly*). Well, you see, there are eleven men on each side, and –

Poppa. As I figger it out, Mr Roberts, this is a contest between the stoodents of two of your great Universities. Now in my country we have one thousand Colleges and Universities, and every one of those institootions is just vi-brating with noo ideas. Now this cricket is not a noo game, I understand, but if it could be introdooced into some of our leading colleges, why, I take it that would be a vurry notable contribution to the friendly relations of your great country and mine. Now, Sir, I should be glad to get your reflexes on that proposition.

Mr Roberts. Well, I think it would be a jolly good thing –

[*Two runs are scored.*]

Mamie (*clapping her hands*). Oh, my Champ! They're getting fresh. Look, there's a man running. Isn't it gay?

Champ (*without enthusiasm*). Yep.

[*A great commotion on the bench behind.* Betty *and* Maud *stand up as* Major Grange *approaches with his niece.*]

Betty (*in a voice that must be clearly audible to every fielder on the on-side*). Well, Major, I thought you were never going to see me. What were you looking at?

Major Grange. Good morning. This is my niece, Phyllis.

Betty. Oh, how d'you do? Will you sit there? No, you sit here and I'll sit there. Now, you sit next to me, Major, and tell me all your news. Now we're all comfortable. Get up, Maud, you're sitting on my purse. No, I can't see anything, and I don't want to. I'm sure I don't know why Maud makes such a fuss about the game. Anyone would think she had a son in the eleven.

1st Enthusiast. Short slip's too fine.

Major Grange (*regarding him darkly*). These young men can't dress themselves nowadays. Soft collars at Lords! Why, I remember when you weren't allowed on the *ground* without a top-hat.

Phyllis (*mildly*). Perhaps they can't afford one, Uncle John.

Major Grange. Too much lawn-tennis nowadays. That's what it is. Effeminate.

Phyllis (*indignant*). I think top-hats are effeminate. Tom doesn't wear one.

Major Grange (*suspicious*). Does he play lawn-tennis?

Phyllis. Of *course!* Everybody does.

Major Grange. Then he's no good. There you are! Clean bowled. I never *saw* such batting.

Betty. Poor boy! He's got a nice figure. Where are you lunching, Major?

Mr Roberts. So, you see, when this side's all out the other side goes in. But if this side makes 150 runs less than the other side, then the other side doesn't go in after all, but *this* side –

Poppa. Did you get that, Mamie? Mr Roberts says when this crowd's through with batting, the other crowd is up against it – that's the crowd standing around in the field right now, I guess – but if the other crowd shows a deficit of 1,500 on the first count, then *this* crowd, that is, the other crowd – Hell, just how did it go, Mr Roberts?

Mr Roberts (*helplessly*). Well, you see, Cambridge made –

Champ. Say, Mr Roberts, that guy that quit batting a while back, what just does he do now?

Mr Roberts. Oh, he just sits in the pavilion.

Poppa (*amazed*). Now you don't tell me, Mr Roberts, that that young fellow is going to sit around in an armchair for the rest of the day?

Mr Roberts. Yes, he will – till his side is out. So will the others – nine of them.

Champ. Gosh! Some game!

Poppa. Well, Sir, you surprise me. Now in my country –

Mamie. Shucks, Poppa! Guess the boy's tired after all that walking.

Poppa. Now in my country we don't figger to have a great amount of sitting down in our national sports. If a young fellow wants to sit down, he can make a reservation at a hotel, but nobody's going to pay dollars to see him do it. No, Sir, we shouldn't stand for *that*.

Betty (*to* Phyllis) My dear, what a pretty frock! *Isn't* it pretty, Maud?

Maud (*engrossed*). What?

Betty. Isn't Miss Grange's frock pretty?

Maud (*turning irritably*). Yes, it's sweetly pretty. (*A wicket falls.*) There, he's out again and I missed it. How was he out?

Major Grange. Caught in the slips.

Phyllis. Bowled.

1st Enthusiast (*turning politely*) Lb.

Betty. Oh, thank you *so* much! Lb. – whatever's that?

Major Grange. Leg-before-wicket. He stopped the ball with his leg.

Betty. The clever boy! Where are you lunching, Major?

Major Grange (*pretending not to hear*). Who's this coming in, Phyllis? Sloppy-looking fellow. I saw young Blakeney yesterday. Off to Wimbledon, if you please – to watch tennis. *Tennis!*

Betty. I quite agree, Major. Wimbledon's dreadful. Nobody speaks a word. That's what I like about Lord's – you can call your soul your own here. Where are you lunching, Major?

Mamie. Pinch me if I snore, Champ.

Mr Roberts (patiently). You see, there are six balls in every over, and at the end of the over a different bowler bowls from the other end – you see?

Poppa. No, Sir, and in my opinion this game will not electrify our great Universities, as a recreation. But it is a vurry remarkable social institootion, and as such deserves the respect of every enlightened American citizen Now, I have a nephew located in Seattle –

1st Enthusiast. Lunch interval! – blow!

Betty. Lunch – at last! I'm famished. Why don't you lunch with us, Major?

Major. Well, I was just going to propose that you came and lunched with *me*, in the Club tent.

Betty. Oh, may we? Delightful! Come along Maud. Now we can talk.

THE BLUE FAIRY-BOOK

One of those foolish men who write for the weekly newspapers recently observed that England is "less generously provided with arresting names" than America. Is she, indeed?

Everybody in the Telephone Book is, of course, a perfect gentleman, and, having once courted publicity by having their names circulated so widely, I am sure the subscribers won't mind my making discreet use of their names to repel this charge.

The other day, for example, as I wandered sadly through the waste of W's, in search for Williams, with what an easing of the soul my eye caught that little oasis on page 914:

"WELLBELOVED A & Sons, Butchrs & Frmrs"

And not one WELLBELOVED only, but at least four! I longed to call the magic number and whisper into the receiver, "O WELLBELOVED, are you there? You have brightened this day for me, WELLBELOVED. Farewell."

But nearly every letter, even the dullest of them, has its romantic relief. When you have waded in vain through the seventh page of that tiresome SMITH family, pass on a page or two. Soothe yourself with the thought that, if you liked, you could have a word with Mr SUNSHINE, JUDAH. Or by simply putting three pennies in the slot and turning the handle, you will be entitled to say, "Hullo! Is that you, PRECIOUS?" or,

"Good morning TREASURE!" or "TRUELOVE, are you there?" "What's in a name?" said SHAKESPEARE, thereby gravely injuring his reputation; for you and I know that nearly everything is in a name. And I should like to ring up Mr LOVELY and ask if I might speak to his daughter. I do *hope* he has a daughter.

There is no THURSDAY in this thrilling book, but there are two men who are MONDAY, and no fewer than five FRIDAYS, four of whom are butchers. But, of course, butchers have much the best taste in names; two of the four WELLBELOVEDS are butchers, and three of the LAVENDERS are butchers; and two of the four PORTWINES belong to the same fastidious trade.

The objection to the Telephone Book is that it makes fantastic works of imagination seem so dull. I mean, when you realize that in this London of ours there are twelve telephone subscribers called STARKEY, and eleven called SMEE... I wonder if the STARKEYS are lucky on the telephone. Or do they moan along the wires, "Wrong number *again*, Miss! O *miserable* STARKEY!"?

The trouble is, I fear, that probably very few of these delightful people really *know* each other. And what marvellous dialogues don't happen in consequence! Can't you imagine them?

"Hullo! Is that you, PLATO? HOMER wants a word with you."

Or:

"Hullo! Is that you, JAPHET, my boy? *Hullo!* This is NOAH.[1]"

Or:

"Hullo, MARS! VENUS speaking."

For all these fine old English names are to be found in the Blue Fairy-Book. How is it one never comes across them in real life? Why does one never see Mr HERBAGE comparing notes with Mr GRASS? Why, oh why have I never been introduced to Mrs SILVERTOP? Or Mrs TWOPENNY? VIRTUE and VICE are both subscribers; but are they in touch?

Perhaps, however, I am wrong. It may be that things are better ordered than I imagine, that every morning GOODLAD has a word with GOODLASS; and Mr BUTTAR has a word with Mr CHEESE; and Mr SOFTLY has a word with Mr YELL; and Mr BUSY murmurs a few hometruths to the Misses IDLE; and MOCK and TURTLE get together.

The prize for the best Literary Name has been awarded, provisionally, to Mr BENJAMIN CRIMP.

The prize for Making the Best of It is awarded to a suburban gentleman, or rather to his parents. Others have been born into the world under the name of Death; but – at least in the Telephone Book – there is only one

DEATH, JOLLY.

It is an impertinent thought; but I wish I had been present when Mr and Mrs Death were deciding what to call the boy.

And now, I suppose, you think I invented them all. Very well, then, look them up yourself.

1. A butcher, of *course*.

BINGO

Since the Armistice my young brother-in-law has been a man of many trades. In the great wave of feeling that swept over the country in December 1918 there was many a patriotic firm prepared to give employment to a good-looking young man who had fought in the Great War and had some capital. For a reasonable investment they were prepared to make him Managing Director, General Secretary, Business Overseer, or any other kind of important officer. Young Tom has been Managing Director to a firm of automobile makers, a firm of bootmakers, a patent medicine concern, and an Accident Insurance Company. He has been all things to all men, and lost his capital in each case.

By a process of elimination his capital has now been entirely eliminated, and when I saw Tom last he was acting as salesman to the Bingo Fire-Extinguisher Company at a purely nominal fee.

As usual, he called on his brother-in-law to do his first deal. I bought the first motorcar; I bought the first pair of boots; I bought the first bottle of NERVO; and I was glad to take out the first Accident Policy, which covered all of them.

Tom bought with him two Bingos, and a dummy Bingo for demonstration purposes – an ugly green bottle on an ugly wooden bracket.

He always takes his business very seriously, and before we had sat down to tea he had begun to tell me about the awful danger of fire. He had had all the latest particulars pumped into him by Mr Pritt, the manager of BINGO.

"The Fire King," he said, "is ever lying in wait for us. Do you realize that nine fires happen *every minute* in the United Kingdom? That means 540 fires every hour, or – 11,960 fires every day – "

"Or 12,960," I suggested. The Fire King had eaten up Tom's arithmetic.

"And I suppose every month there are practically 388,800 fires," I went on, "and in a normal year you would have as many as 4,399,200?"

I was appalled. The thing had got hold of me.

"That's right," he said solemnly. "And the awful thing is this: If everybody had a BINGO half those fires would never have happened. There'd have been no need to call in the Fire Brigade." He leaned forward and tapped me on the knee. "*At any moment you may have a fire in this house.*"

"Good God!" I said, and I knocked out my pipe.

"Now Bingo's not an ordinary thing," he said. "It's made of a special chemical – "

"What's that?"

"Well, it's – Pritt told me it was – damn it – it's bi – di – tri – bisulphate, or something."

"Peroxide, perhaps?"

"No it's not that."

"Permanganate of potash – lead oxide – sulphuretted hydrogen?"

"Yes, it's one of those. Now I want you to buy three – one for each floor. You fasten it to the wall – like this." George held the dummy Bingo over the mantelpiece between two Japanese prints. It did not look well "When an outbreak of fire is noticed in the house," he continued, "you simply seize the bottle, and tear it from the bracket – like this – thus removing the stopper." Tom seized the bottle and tore it from the mantelpiece, removing the Japanese prints; and the china shepherdess, but not the stopper.

"What do I do now?"

"You fling it into the heart of the flame," said Tom with enthusiasm "By the way, this bottle's tremendously *strong*. Pritt says you can open a packing-case with it – "

"Is that a good thing?"

Tom paid no attention. "It's like no other extinguisher on the market. You can poke the fire with it! You can hammer in nails with it! You *can't break* it!" he cried.

"But I thought the whole idea of a fire-extinguisher was that it *would* break?"

"Not at all," said Tom; and in his eyes was a holy light. "I can throw it on the floor – thus – and – "

George threw the dummy Bingo violently upon the floor. It broke into a thousand pieces.

We gazed at the pieces in profound silence.

Tom scratched his head ruefully. "I made sure I'd got that piece about the packing-case right. This must be a faulty sample."

"Perhaps it was," I agreed. "Try poking the fire with one of the others."

The light came back into his eyes. "Of *course!*" he said; and seizing the second Bingo he thrust it into the grate, and heaved the coals about. As far as I could see the experiment was strikingly successful. The bottle did not appear to break, but there was a blue flash, and a great tongue of flame shot out into the room. Tom jumped back hastily, and I smelt the smell of singeing. In the grate there was an angry blaze. Columns of black smoke rolled up the chimney. If I had not seen Tom put the fire-extinguisher in it, I should have said that the fire was on fire. He thought so too, apparently. For "Quick!" he cried, "the other one!" He seized the third Bingo and tore it from the bracket, according to directions. This time the stopper duly removed itself, and Tom impetuously poured the whole pint of peroxide on the heart of the flames. There was another blinding flash, and the heart of the flames dilated into a roaring furnace. The heat was terrific. The room was filled with suffocating smoke. Choking, we withdrew to the door. The two armchairs beside the hearth caught fire. I tottered to the telephone and coughed an urgent call for the Fire Brigade.

Afterwards, the firemen said that they had never known a fire of such small beginnings endure with such obstinacy. The flames had some peculiar quality in them; the more hoses you turned on them, the more fiercely they blazed. As we walked away from the ruins of my house Tom said, cheerfully enough in the circumstances, "That's the worst of these damned samples." And I said, very cheerfully, I think "Anyhow, we've broken the record."

"What do you mean?"

"This year there will be 4,399,20*1* fires."

THE ADVOWSONEER

"Them advowsons is funny things," said Sir William Bunlip, KBE, rolling his friendly forget-me-not eyes across the links. "Did you ever 'ave one?"

"No," said I. "I used to keep newts, and once I had a salamander – but it died."

"Advowsons isn't animals," said Sir William in a superior tone. "It's religion. Won't you 'ave a drink?"

"Yes," said I. I do not often golf at Goldbridge-*prope*-London but when I do I am ready for any devilry. I like to sit on the verandah before lunch and watch the rich men recovering from their round, drinking in the peerless English air and the priceless Italian Vermouth. And that morning I had had a wearing game behind two extremely seedy and unskilful youths, whom we "went through," not without unpleasantness at the thirteenth.

"I see a piece in *Punch* about 'em not long ago," said Sir William, "but the feller didn't know what he was talking about. All the same 'e did me a good turn," said the Red Knight. "Well, 'ere's luck. Funny sort of gin, this. You see, I've been collectin' advowsons a long time."

"By the way, what *is* an advowson?" I enquired innocently.

"An advowson is the right of presentin' a parson to a spirituous livin'. And you can buy 'em in the open market, like you can manor-'ouses and Old Masters, and all that. Well, I've been collectin' 'em ever since I retired after the War. I did my bit, like the rest of us, as perhaps you know."

"Yes," I said with emotion.

"Well, I wanted somethin' to do," he went on. "Most men 'as an 'obby of some kind when they retire. Sometimes it's butterflies, sometimes it's beer; or cut-glass. Mine's advowsons. First I bought slowly – I 'ad to. You see, it's like manor-'ouses – these things belongs to a lot of stuck-up landed gentry – "

"Swine," said I.

"You're right – swine, some of them – and I 'ad to go careful. But they're feelin' the breeze, my boy, they're feelin' the breeze. I keep a good lawyer, and what they wouldn't sell to me man-to-man they'll sell to a lawyer with a good name through the three-'alfpenny post. Any'ow, in three years, one way an' another, I collected about twenty, some 'ere, some there, some rich, some pore, but all good stuff. I don't buy trash. And I'll lay you any odds there isn't another man in this country 'as twenty first-chop spirituous livin's to give away. There's one in the West of England, now – sixteenth-century church, vicarage as large as this club-'ouse, fat income, old parson dyin' in a year or two, and I don't know 'ow many acres of globe – "

"Glebe?" I suggested diffidently.

"Glebe – you've 'it it. Well, then, this writin'-feller puts 'is piece in the paper about advowsons, and since that there's been 'igh old doin's on the market. I don't know if you read the Agony column in *The Times*?"

"I don't read much else," said I.

"Same 'ere," said Sir William. "I was never much of a one for books myself. But I know a good advow. when I see it, and just lately there's been a 'ole flood of 'em goin', I've got one 'ere." And he handed me a cutting from *The Times*.

I read:

SEALYHAM BITCH for sale. Warranted...

TO LET, FURNISHED – BIJOU FLAT...

ADVOWSON – For Sale, the Advowson of a living in – ; income, chiefly tithe, about £850 net; fine church, large vicarage, small town; present incumbent over 75 years of age; good garden. – Q. 890.

"I've enquired about that," said Sir William. "The lawyer says the old man's aged and feeble – might pip any day. But I mean to run down an' 'ave a look at 'im before I buy. I don't trust these parsons. The other day," he went on, "there was six in one add. *I bought the lot!*"

"Well done," said I. "Have another drink?"

"Well, I don't mind if I do – another of the same, only more gin. You see these landed stuck-ups 'ave been feelin' the breeze for some time, as I told you. But just now they've got the wind up proper. You see it's a funny sort of a thing, when you come to think of it, all these advow-thingummies bein' bought and sold in a daily paper like furnished flats – only most people don't know nothin' about it and care less. But that piece in the paper was fit to frighten a military 'orse, and these fellows *is* frightened. They think per'aps one day there'll be trouble in the 'Ouse of Commons and the Government'll step in and kick 'em out. So they're sellin' out while they can. *And I'm buyin'*. 'Ere's luck!"

"The Fates preserve you!" said I heartily. "But what *good* does it do you?"

"Well," said Sir William, "for one thing it's a 'obby, as I told you, and cheap as 'obbies go. You can get a first-class, 'Ome Counties, old-established advow for a couple of thou or less. And, for another thing, it's my experience that you never lose by cornerin' a market. The Government might kick these tinpot squires out for nothin', but they won't kick William Bunlip out for nothin' – see? And I could afford it if they did. Besides, I'm a man with a lot of nephews on my 'ands – "

"Excuse me, Sir," said a voice at my elbow and, looking round, I saw dear old Phineas P Sexton, of Chicago, who has been having a few games at the club – "excuse me, Sir," he said, "but right here is where I'd be reel glad to butt in, if you'll pardon the liberty – "

I introduced the two.

"How do?" said Sir William.

"Glad to know you, Sir," said Phineas. "Now, Sir, I couldn't help hearing some of the powerful exposition you've been giving of your old English customs. I'm a collector myself. In my home on Michigan Avenue I have two first editions of the poet KEATS, one genuine GAINSBOROUGH, and a lock of hair from the head of LORD NELSON. But I've not gotten one of these ad-what-is-its – no, Sir, not any. And I'd be tickled to death to take one home with me to Mrs Sexton in the *Carbolic* next week. See here, Sir, I'll give you fifty thousand dollars for that crackerjack you were mentioning in the Middle West. Is it a deal, Sir?"

"It is not," said Sir William. "I'm sorry "

"I'll make it sixty thousand – seventy! I have a cheque here, and I'm crazy to get it. Name your own figure, Sir."

"No," said Sir William, "I won't sell that one. I'd like to oblige you, and there's a little one in Lincolnshire you could 'ave for nothing, and another one in the North – but not Fishton. Don't think me mean, Mr Sexton. I've got my reasons. And 'ere they are."

Just then the two seedy young golfers tottered in from the last green.

Sir William called to the seedier of the two.

"Well, Walter, 'oo won the game?"

"I did, Uncle," said Walter.

"Then that settles it," said Sir William. "Mr Sexton, these are two of my nephews. This is Walter – Walter Bunlip, the future Vicar of Fishton. And this is Stanley – and now 'e'll 'ave to be content with Little Mugberry."

FRANÇOIS

Life is not entirely denuded of romance. To this day you can buy an Italian lizard in Shaftesbury Avenue and give him the freedom of your garden to run about in the sun and eat your insects in the Italian manner. Surely a good thing to do.

But when I rescued Antonio I also rescued François, who was one of those jolly little French tree-frogs. I call them French because I have been to France and I saw one there. But any friend of mine who has been to Italy looks at them and says, "Oh, yes, they have those in Italy"; and any friend who has been to Spain says, "Oh, yes, the Spanish frog." Anyhow, they have the true Continental vivacity and are most attractive, not like your oily lumbering English frog, but tiny and dry to the touch and painted a beautiful vivid green.

Well, we walked down to Covent Garden Station, the three of us; at least I walked and the others rode. They rode in a nice tin-can, with holes in the top, and naturally we were all rather elated, for it was no weather for living in Shaftesbury Avenue, even if you were accustomed to the hot suns of Italy, or France, or Spain. But when I sat down in the train naturally I just raised the lid of the tin the tiniest fraction; not to look at my companions, of course, but merely to let them know that everything was going well and we shouldn't be long now, and they mustn't excite themselves.

Just the tiniest fraction, but...

One of these days there will be a new Underground poster. It will say:

DO NOT BUY YOUR
LIZARDS
DURING THE RUSH-HOURS.

Yes, Antonio did the unpardonable thing. He darted out like green lightning and traversed the persons of four different people before any of them had time to scream; then paused on a well-developed lady who clearly, like myself, had been committing the sin of shopping between five and six. She carried a large basket of grapes, and no doubt it was this familiar fruit which caused Antonio to halt where he did and not on the city man next to her. He halted on the lady's shoulder, slipping his little black tongue in and out in a perfectly friendly way.

Unfortunately he did not stay there. With the marvellous instinct of animals he began to dislike the stout lady as much as I did, and even sooner; and he darted off again.

The human mind moves strangely in an emergency. During the desperate scene that followed, two thoughts occupied most of mine: (*a*) I seemed to have heard somewhere that a lizard, if over-excited, is capable of discarding his tail as a protest, and I had a hideous fear that Antonio would make this gesture, and make it probably on the stout lady; (*b*) I remembered vividly the leading case of *Rylands* v. *Fletcher*, which decided (as, of course, you know) that, if a man keeps a wild beast or a reservoir or a bad smell on his property, and it escapes on to his neighbour's through no fault of his own, he is responsible for the consequences. And I kept wondering whether *Rylands* v. *Fletcher* would cover a lizard on the Tube.

I had no doubt that the stout lady would bring an action, for shock or what-not. I could tell that by her scream.

Let us not dwell on these moments. Enough to say that Antonio was caught at last, tail intact, and the panic subsided.

And now imagine me, standing meekly in the middle of the crowded compartment clutching the tin like a bomb in danger of bursting, and suffering a barbarous cross-fire of remarks.

Perfectly just remarks – I admit it. Still, they were remarks. The stout lady's were the worst. She said that Antonio was poisonous. And she said something subtle about "reptiles."

Anyhow, we are both sensitive creatures, and after a station or two of this we determined to leave the inhospitable train and take another.

And then – it must have been about Dover Street – my blood ran cold.

I saw François.

He must have escaped during the pursuit of Antonio.

These frogs have extraordinary climbing powers, very prehensile paws, and a love of being on an eminence, however slight. François had raised himself to an eminence. He was perched upon a maiden's hat, quite still, staring at an advertisement.

The maiden was not three feet from me, but there was a man between us. I opened my mouth, I moved my arm...and I did nothing.

Now what would *you* have done? Remembering all that had gone before, would you, at the risk of perhaps another panic, of more remarks, of *Rylands* v. *Fletcher* – would you have stretched out your hand across a strange shoulder and remarked to a strange though pleasant-looking maiden, "Excuse me, that's my frog"? Would you really?

You lie.

Or would you have slipped out of the train at Hyde Park Corner and abandoned François to his fate? *Never!*

I began edging towards the maiden, hoping for a chance to recapture François in some more secret manner.

At Earl's Court I was still edging.

Imagine, if you can, my sensations during that terrible period. François looked cool and collected enough, but at the best, anyone might see him at any moment and raise the alarm. Worse, at any moment he might take a wild leap and land upon some other lady. If that happened I knew that the great case of *The Stout Lady* v. *Me* would never be called. I should be lynched.

At Earl's Court the maiden was swept out of the train and bolted up the moving staircase. I followed. We just caught a Putney train. I did not want to go to Putney. I never want to go to Putney. But I followed.

I began edging again.

At Putney Bridge she got out. I followed. I followed her up the hill. What would you have done? Would you have let that poor girl go home in ignorance and have hysterics when she took off her hat? Never. Besides, I wanted François.

She glanced behind her with suspicion as she walked, and once, passing a policeman, she seemed about to stop. I prepared to be arrested.

But she went on. I was close behind her now, steadily plucking up courage; and at last she turned and faced me.

"Why are you following me?" she demanded.

Then I said the impossible thing. "I beg your pardon, but you've got a frog of mine in your hat."

Superb creature! Not a shriek, not a shiver. She simply smiled in a curious way and said, "Oh! I'm very sorry. Please take it."

I raised my hand and, coyly enough, took hold of François.

There were green leaves like water-lilies on the hat, and the little thing looked quite at home. In fact, he clung on firmly with his prehensile paws, as if reluctant to be moved.

He *was* reluctant. He would not come.

Then the maiden began to giggle. "Don't pinch him," she said; "he's only celluloid."

Antonio and François are both doing well in the garden.

A LITTLE RIOT

I am one of those men who always know immediately what I think about everything. I have judgment and decision. Like some of the papers. I know at once whether a man is a Bolshevist or a Patriot. And I say so.

I am also a man of unusual personal courage.

So when I heard that a riot had been arranged to take place in Trafalgar Square I deliberately stayed in Trafalgar Square. I stayed near the entrance to the subway to the Tube.

I distrust the partisan accounts of riots. I distrust the Communist papers when they say that the capitalist police made a brutal and unprovoked assault on the demonstrators, felled three women, and threw a baby under an omnibus.

I distrust the other papers when they say that half the Unemployed had obviously been working, full time for the past six months, and the remaining half were obviously alien enemies who had never worked at all and never would.

It was time for an impartial observer to observe a riot and discover the truth. I stood by my burrow and admired the scene. It was dusk. Trafalgar Square was beautiful and dim in a blue haze. The lights came out in the shops. Lord Nelson melted slowly into the mist. I reflected on him. The lions grew black and very large. Someone told me once that all the ground under the Nelson Column and under the lions and under the fountains and under the National Gallery is occupied by vast wine-cellars. I reflected on that.

The Man About Town

I admired the policemen, the calm magnificent men; I admired their horses, shiny and magnificent, but not so calm. (What is it they put on horses to make them shine so?) The policemen have all put on an expression of calm to make the public think that nothing is going to happen. As I reflect on this, the rumour spreads that the rioters are approaching from the NW.

A crowd collects, waiting for the riot to begin. The man next to me tells me that if I keep moving I shall not be arrested. So we keep moving. We move round and round the railings of the subway entrance, followed by a huge policeman. It is like Musical Chairs. It is awful when we are on the far side, away from the steps; I feel sure that I shall be caught on that side when the music stops – or rather when the band begins to play. But my friend tells me that if I stop still for a moment I shall be arrested at sight. I am afraid he is a Bolshevist. But he is rather a nice one. He seems to like me. He takes me for a Bolshevist.

It is no good. I cannot move on any more. I am going to stand still. Now I shall be arrested.

The huge policeman is looking at me severely. A nice man. He is not going to arrest me after all. He seems to like me. He takes me for a Patriot.

Down the road comes the procession, cheering aggressively. They have been told they cannot have a meeting in the Square. They have been meeting for three hours in Hyde Park already. From my experience of meetings that should be enough for any man. Why should they have another meeting here, blocking the traffic on a week-day? Especially when they have been told not to… I am for Law and Order.

But why not let them meet in the Square? They can't say anything redder than they said in the Park. And it is my experience that meetings obstruct traffic much less thoroughly than riots. I am for common sense.

Thank heaven, I know what I think about things.

The procession has become a Mob. The Mob has broken through the policemen. They have mounted the – what is it? – the lintel? – the plinth. They are booing unpleasantly at the policemen. They have raised the Red Flag. It is the Revolution. It is all up.

The poor policemen! I'm sorry for them. It is humiliating. My Bolshevist is delighted. He says they will never get "the boys" out of the Square now. There are too many.

"The boys" are being turned off the plinth by two policemen. They go very rapidly. It is not the Revolution after all.

There is a poor old Englishman arguing with my policeman. He is not a good arguer. He is almost crying. He says, "Why *shouldn't* I go in there? It's a place of recreation, ain't it?" The policeman says, "Gerralong outerthis," and pushes him with a huge hand. I am a Bolshevist.

A dirty little alien is yowling like a wild cat at my policeman. I am a Patriot.

There is an ugly temper abroad; but nobody seems to know exactly what to do next. I am in an ugly temper too, but I know exactly what to do. I must get round these railings to the subway entrance; for I was caught on the wrong side. I knew it would happen.

Everybody about me is yowling aimlessly. My Bolshevist says suddenly, "Gaw! them something 'orses!" and bolts for the Tube. The horses are charging.

I stand firm. They are charging in the opposite direction There they go, the calm magnificent men. They have drawn those terrible long staves, truncheons, or batons. They are hitting people on the head with them They have knocked down an old man – the old man I saw just now. Shame! They have knocked down another man – the dirty little alien. Capital!

Why do they hit people on the head? Those shiny horses are surely enough to make a man a Patriot.

They are enough for *me*. Goodness! they are charging this way. I am off. I surrender. I will read the *Morning Post* – I promise.

I am down the steps. I am underground. Thank heaven! Now I am a Bolshevist again. Surely no horse will follow me down the subway.

Here is my Bolshevist friend again. We peer through the bottom of the railings at the flying hoofs of the policemen's horses. They strike fire from the pavement. It is picturesque – from underground.

I see two policemen with their heads cut open. Broken bottles! Ugh! No wonder they hit people on the head. I wonder if they hit the right man.

My friend says, "Ain't you glad you was born in England?" I answer "Yes." He thinks I am ironical. He is pleased.

It is all over. The mob is cowed. I am cowed. We creep out. The Square is clear. We creep home. Wherever I creep there is a policeman on a huge horse. I cower in the doorway of a jeweller's shop. A policeman says "Move on there"; and he waves a hand to direct me towards the stern end of six other horses strung across the pavement. Policemen's horses are never supposed to kick or to tread on one's toes. I know that. But do the horses know it? I enter the jeweller's shop. I want to buy a diamond ring.

I emerge, having bought nothing. I creep home. I am glad I have discovered the truth. I am glad I know what I think about it all.

Do you?

THE LITTLE HORSE

[The following fragment is taken from the play, *David Lloyd George*, which was written in the days of the Coalition, as a companion-piece to *Abraham Lincoln*.]

The scene is laid in the House of Commons, where Sir Frederick Banbury has moved the rejection of the Art (Reorganization) Bill. Sir Frederick Banbury is speaking.

    But it stands to reason,
    If you propose to pay them just the same
    Whether they paint a little or a lot,
    They won't paint *anything*. There will not be
    Sufficient stimulus. It's human nature,
    And human nature is unchangeable.
    Do you imagine, Sir, that WATTS or TURNER
    Would have produced such valuable work,
    So large an output, if this precious Bill
    Had been in operation at the time?
    Besides, it means the death of British Art,
    Because we can't continue to compete
    With foreign countries.
A Labour Member.   I am not a lawyer
    Nor I am not a manufacturer,
    But earned my bread these five-and-forty years,
    Sweating and sweating. I know what sweat is…

The Man About Town

An Hon. Member.
   You're not the only person who has sweated.
Labour Member.
   At any rate I sweated more than you did.
Mr Speaker.
   I do not think these constant interruptions
   Are really helping us.
Labour Member.   So you may take it
   That what I utter is an honest word,
   A plain, blunt, honest, and straightforward word,
   Neither adorned with worthless flummery
   And tricks of language – for I have no learning –
   Nor yet with false and empty rhetoric
   Like lawyers' speeches. I am not a lawyer,
   I thank my God that I am not a lawyer,
   And can without a spate of parleying
   Briefly expound, as I am doing now,
   The whole caboodle. As for this here Bill,
   So far as it means Nationalising Art,
   We shall support it. On the other hand,
   So far as it means interferences
   With the free liberty of working-men
   To paint their pictures when and how they like,
   We will not *have* the Bill. So now you know.
Mr Asquith.
   It was remarked, I think by ARISTOTLE,
   That wisdom is not always to the wise;
   To which opinion, if we may include
   In that august and jealous category
   The President of the Board of Education,
   I am prepared most freely to subscribe.
   When was there ever since the early 'Forties
   A more grotesque or shameless mockery
   Of the austere and holy principles
   Which Liberalism like an altar-flame

Has guarded through the loose irreverent years
Than this inept, this disingenuous,
This frankly disingenuous attempt
To smuggle past the barrier of this House
An article so plainly contraband
As this unlicensed and contagious Bill –
A Bill which, it is not too much to say,
Affronts the conscience of the British Empire?
I will not longer, Sir, detain the House;
Indeed, I cannot profitably add
To what I said in 1892.
Speaking at Manchester I used these words:
"If in the inconstant ferment of their minds
The KING'S advisers can indeed discover
No surer ground of principle than this;
If we have here their final contribution
To the most clamant and profound conundrum
Ever proposed for statesmanship to solve,
Then are we watching at the bankruptcy
Of all that wealth of intellect and power
Which has made England great. If that be true
We may put FINIS to our history.
But I for one will never lend my suffrage
To that conclusion."

[*An Ovation.*]

Mr David Lloyd George.   Mr SPEAKER, Sir,
I do not intervene in this discussion
Except to say how much I deprecate
The intemperate tone of many of the speakers –
Especially the Honourable Member
For Always Dithering – about this Bill,
This tiny Bill, this teeny-weeny Bill
What is it, after all? The merest trifle!
The merest trifle – no, not tipsy-cake –
No trickery in it! Really one would think

The Man About Town

The Government had nothing else to do
But sit and listen to offensive speeches.
How can the horse, the patient horse, go on
If people will keep dragging at the reins?
He has so terrible a load to bear,
And right in front there is a great big hill.
The horse is very tired, and it is raining.
Poor little horse! But yonder, at the top,
Look, look, there is a rainbow in the sky,
The promise of fair weather, and beyond
There is a splendidly-appointed stable,
With oats and barley, or whatever it is
That horses eat, while smiling all around
Stretch out the Prairies of Prosperity,
Cornfields and gardens, all that sort of thing.
That's where the horse is going. But, you see,
The horse has got to climb the great big hill
Before he gets there. Oh, you must see that.
Then let us cease this petty bickering;
Let us have no more dragging at the reins.
What *is* this Bill when all is said and done?
Surely this House, surely this mighty nation,
Which did so much for horses in the War,
Will not desert this little horse at last
Because of what calumniators say –
Newspaper-owners – *I* know who they are –
About this Bill! No, no, of course it won't.
We will take heart and gallop up the hill,
We will climb up together to the rainbow;
We will go on to where the rainbow ends –
I know where that is, for I am a Welshman.
I know a field, a lovely little field,
Where there are buttercups and daffodils,
And long rich grass and very shady trees.
Hold on a little, and the horse will get there,

Only, I ask you, let the horse have rein.
That is my message to the British nation:
"Hold on! Hold fast! But do not hold too tight!"
    [*An Ovation. A Division is taken. The Ayes have it.*]

CORAL ISLAND

(*A Novel for the Film*)

CHAPTER I "UP ANCHOR"

It was sunset in the little harbour of Rumble, and the sloop *White Witch* was getting under way. The anchor was hove short, and in the catheads stood a young girl, busy with the pawl. The jib was already hoisted, and as

MARION TARVER

stepped aside to avoid being flung into the water by the flapping sail one saw that her hair was of pure gold.

By the mast stood a young Englishman, clean-limbed, limber, and slim! and now he hauled on the throat halyard, which was jammed in the jaws of the gaff, and now on the peak halyard, which was foul of the topping-lift.

"Anchor's a-trip," cried the girl; and "Hell!" replied her husband. For

JOHN TARVER

had that day taken Marion to wife in the little church upon the hill. And now, on the first of the ebb, they were putting out upon the sea of life. In this frail craft (fifteen tons displacement and forty feet over all) they were to voyage round the world and see strange things.

How strange they little knew.

THE SPIRIT OF DRAKE

And now they were away, these two, alone upon the ocean. The Needles light bore NE by E^3/$_4$E astern. The *White Witch* bounded down the Channel of Old England, griping a little, for she carried too much weather-helm. The girl sat at the tiller, her hair like spun gold in the last rays of the setting sun.

"I have forgotten the charts," said John at last, as he re-spoke his love. "We must go back."

"What matter?" cried the fearless girl. "There must be no turning back.

LOVE IS OUR CHART."

Their lips met.
A squall carried away the topsail.
"Luff," he said simply.

CHAPTER II SHIPWRECK

With a gesture of despair the man turned away from his contemplation of the empty sea, and his eye ranged for the thousandth time the yellow shore, empty also but for a few stray snapping turtles, salamanders, sea-frogs, and tropical newts. He was in rags, and his face bore the marks of hardship and suffering: but one could see that once, at least, he had been a clean-limbed, limber young Englishman. His head ached, and he could not think clearly. His foot struck a broken spar on which was painted in large letters the words *White Witch*. He stared at it, uncomprehending. The words struck no answering chord of memory. What was the *White Witch*? And who, for the matter of that, was he? He remembered nothing but a tremendous concussion. Before that ALL WAS BLANK. He knew now that he was alone on the island. He had walked all round it, hallooing. No one had answered.

At that moment there was a rustle in the undergrowth of yams and upas-trees which fringed the shore. And there emerged on all fours a most beautiful girl. Her hair was like spun gold. She was dressed quite simply in the main-sheet of the *White Witch*, skilfully worked into a dress with torn fragments of the storm-jib, stitched together with pine needles.

She stared at him, frightened; and his face seemed to strike no answering chord of memory.

"Who are you?" he said.

"I do not know," she answered. "I have lost my memory."

"So have I."

"I heard you hallooing," she said, "but I was afraid to halloo back."

His jaw set.

"You NEED HAVE NO FEAR," he said.

She held out her hand with a frank gesture.

"PALS, EH?" she said.

"Pals," he replied.

CHAPTER III CALM

That night he built her a rude hut with the trunks of catalpa-trees, flanked by great boulders which he carried from the shore, and lashed together with tarred string and reef-points from the wreckage of the *White Witch*. The roof was of raw hide, the property of two buck wapiti, which he killed by the power of the human eye and a few bad words in common use at sea. Over the whole he put two coats of boat-varnish and a layer of pitch. In three hours the hut was ready.

Himself, he slept rough in the long grass outside. It rained.

CHAPTER IV PALS

The days slipped by. Boy and girl, like brother and sister, they did together the busy and exhausting work of an island, sharing its disappointments, its simple pleasures, as comrades, as companions, as pals.

The little camp grew. On the second day he built a laundry for her, diverting a river for the supply of water. On the third he built a cookhouse, and constructed a rough oven out of an old anchor. On the fourth he caught two mountain goats, and built a dairy. By the sixth day they seemed to lack nothing, and he sat down and thought.

Meanwhile, Marion was not idle. Milking the goats, feeding the turtles (she was very fond of animals) – always she sang at her work; and all day her bell-like voice was heard booming across the island. One day she rescued a young turtle which had ventured out of its depth.

Two things only disturbed the even tenor of their thoughts. They could not remember who they were. And no one came to take them away.

And every night John slept rough in the long grass, protecting his pal. And nearly always it rained.

CHAPTER V DEEP WATER

One day, wandering through the forest with his home-made axe, the man caught sight of his reflection in a stream, and stood appalled. He had grown a beard.

Without hesitation he diverted the stream. And on the way home he hacked off the beard

"Why have you done that?" said the woman at late dinner. "I do not know," he replied, avoiding her frank gaze

The next day she crept out to the stream and looked in it. What she saw there amazed her She had not known that she was beautiful. She had forgotten all that. But her nose was shining.

She went back thoughtfully, and powdered her nose with a little flour which she had made from the bread-fruit. She did not know why she did this.

NATURE, THE GREAT TEACHER

That night, as John looked at her across the yams, some hidden chord of his being seemed to vibrate. He glanced at her curiously. She wore the same frock still, and by now the main-sheet was sadly frayed; yet there was a something –

What was it?

"Pal," he said,

"YOU LOOK DIFFERENT TONIGHT

What have you done?"

She made no reply. There are some secrets that must be forever hidden from man, deep-locked in woman's breast.

"Tell me about your work," she said softly.

"Today," he said, "I built a beacon on Prospect Point. Tomorrow – but there, I'm boring you."

"Go on," she said gently. "Somehow I feel that one day you will do something much bigger than – than all this, something bigger than you have ever done."

Their eyes met. And suddenly he knew that they were Man and Woman – boy and girl no longer. And he loved her – loved her

WITH EVERY FIBRE OF HIS BEING.

His pulses drummed. Come what might, she should never know.

The next day he cut down the greater part of the forest, and built a ten-foot stockade about the hut.

"Why have you done that?" she asked.

"Snakes," he said evasively.

CHAPTER VI RED SKIES

Day by day the man worked harder. He had built a dam, a breakwater, three cairns, and a semaphore. He had built a rough furnace and a rough harbour. Then from the hollow trunk of the banyan he began to build a rough boat. But this he kept from the woman. All day he worked with his hands, hoping thus to occupy his mind; and in the evening he spoke in loud tones, lest the drumming of his pulses should betray him.

Work! work! If he did not work he knew that one day he would blurt out

THE GHASTLY SECRET

of his love.

Sometimes he threw stones at her to conceal his passion.

How he worked! He gave names to every promontory, stream, and gully in the island. Along the hill-tops ran a chain of beacons, cairns and rough signalling stations. Huts and workshops dotted the shore. The forest had nearly disappeared. The whole face of the island was changed.

Thus once again in the long struggle between Man and Nature, man had been victorious.

And secretly the boat advanced.

One day he cut down the last tree and made a rough mast with it. From the bark he made a rude sail. The boat was ready. And now there was nothing more that he could do. With no manual labour to occupy him he would be forced to speak his love. Unless the boat…

He walked twice round the island, renaming the promontories.

He looked out to sea. There was nothing to be seen, nothing but coral reefs and the black fins of sharks. The island, like so many of its kind, was off the trade routes. This boat was their only hope…

He pushed the boat into the water. It sank immediately.

And now there was no way out – none.

He looked out to sea again. But yes, there *was* a way out.

LIFE – OR HONOUR?

CHAPTER VII JETTISON

The woman was in the library, reading a rough book which he had made for her.

"I am going away," he said simply. "You will be safe now. I have killed the snake. If you should see a sail, depress the lever in Prospect Valley and twenty beacons will be immediately ignited. Goodbye."

"Where are you going?" she said.

"I judge that we are no great distance from some Continent or other," he replied. "I go to bring help."

"Can I not go with you?"

"THE BOAT WILL NOT HOLD TWO," he said evasively.

"I do not fear death," she said.

"I go to save you from

WORSE THAN DEATH."

"You are a very brave man," she answered wondering.

"Goodbye, pal," he said and, turning on his heel, strode down to the shore.

She gave a choking cry,

" — !"

But he did not turn his head. And even now she could not reveal the secret he so little suspected.

East and West, from Piccadilly to the far Pacific,

A WOMAN'S HEART

is the same.

CHAPTER VIII SALVAGE

When she saw him stride into the sea she guessed at once his desperate design. He intended to swim to the nearest Continent. At all costs he must be stopped. It was too far.

She ran down and followed him through the clear blue tropical water. The turtles scattered before her, uttering their curious flute-like cries. And suddenly she realised that she could not swim.

He was far out now, swimming strongly with both arms. But what was that, away to the west, black and sinister and flashing in the sun? Her blood ran cold. It was the fin of a shark.

Something nudged her. It was Tulip, her favourite turtle, nosing for food; Tulip whose child she had befriended.

Quick as thought she jumped upon his back, and whispering in his ear urged the huge creature after her unsuspecting pal.

The intelligent beast seemed to realise that something was required of him and plied his flippers with a will.

And now began a grim race. The shark was swift, but he had farther to go; and Tulip was the fleetest turtle in all the Pacific.

Still the shark gained rapidly. Now he was close astern, and Marion could feel his hot breath on her shoulder. Leaning back she struck the cruel monster a stinging blow in the face with her open hand.

The shark bit his lip, reddening at the insult.

But the moment's delay was priceless. In an instant the man had vaulted on to the back of the turtle, and Tulip, with his double freight, was paddling briskly for the shore.

The shark, with a snarl of baffled rage, headed out to sea and was never seen again.

CHAPTER IX HAVEN

Their lips met.

CHAPTER X TEMPTATION

Athwart the coral reef the blue sea murmured listlessly. The moon rose out of the ocean like some great sphere. The hum of the salamander thrilled languorous in the distance; and somewhere could be heard the sensuous cheeping of an axolotl.

They were alone with Nature.

The man's brow darkened. He tore himself from her arms.

"You did wrong to save my life," he said; "our lips must not meet again."

"We are alone with Nature," she replied. "We have flung off the artificial trappings of the world we knew. Before heaven we are man and wife."

"WHERE THERE IS NO SOCIETY THERE CAN BE NO SIN."

"Sin is not the product of society," he answered, "it concerns the soul."

Somewhere in the undergrowth a chipmunk mewed, calling to his mate. Along the chequered sand the fireflies glowed, lighting in a thousand windows

THE LAMPS OF LOVE.

But he – there came into his mind dim pictures of the past.

The playing-fields at Eton... Roll-Call... The Terrace of the House of Commons... His mother...

He did not know what these pictures were, or whence they came. But the figures in them, so noble and gracious, seemed to be speaking to him a message from a world which he did not remember in a language which he did not understand.

Ah, the pitiless irony of Fate! For it is written: Man may build bridges out of a dead tree, but he cannot at will construct a parson.

"Life without Honour is an empty thing," he said simply, "Good night."

All night he roamed the island, renaming the promontories for the third time.

CHAPTER XI INTERMEZZO

Years passed.

CHAPTER XII MONSOON

How she bored him!

CHAPTER XIII NOCTURNE

How he bored her!

CHAPTER XIV THE DOLDRUMS

The dull conventional routine of the island. The way he killed snakes, over and over again… The way she did her hair. Her cooking…

CHAPTER XV THE RESCUE

And in the morning a great steamer lay in the bay, calling for water.

Captain Sampson, hard-bitten, upright weather-beaten, type of the men who keep our ships afloat and our flag aflutter, looked John Tarver in the eyes.

"Before we weigh anchor for the white cliffs of England," he said, "I will ask you a straight question: What are your relations with this woman?"

John Tarver hung his head.

"Seven years ago," he said, "I kissed her on the lips."

A spasm of disgust passed over the tarred face before him.

"Put him in irons," said the Captain.

CHAPTER XVI SCHEHEREZADE

The giant liner pounded over the ocean, eating up the miles. On the promenade-deck the richer passengers idled away their time with card-games and quoits. Butterflies...

And down in the bilge John Tarver gnawed at his irons, alone with his shame. What a contrast! But he had broken the Unwritten Code of decent men, and he must pay the score. Ostracised by the first-class passengers, who pointedly shunned the hold in which he lay – but, Pah! he cared nothing for them. One face only rose in the gloom before him.

But with every revolution of the screw the day drew nearer when he would be handed over to the proper authorities at Southampton. He would never see her again.

Almost angrily he brushed the rats from his sleeve.

And on the bridge Captain Sampson passionately pressed his suit.

For a moment Marion was drawn by his rugged honesty and the glamour of his calling. He showed her the compass. He explained the Theory of the Tides.

"Be mine," he said," and I will let you hold the wheel."

She was tempted.

Then there rose before her the image of the man who had shared so many perils with her; and she re-thrilled to the old spell.

"Captain," she said, "the day we cross the bar I will give you my reply."

Dark clouds were massing to windward.
"The glass is falling," he said grimly.

CHAPTER XVII TORNADO

The great ship was in the grip of a hurricane. In all his forty years at sea the Captain could not remember a wind of such velocity. Crouched behind the dodger, with all his skill he baffled the elements. The huge vessel quivered. The swimming-bath was closed. The squash-racquets competition was postponed. The frightened passengers clustered in the rigging.

And how fared it with the lonely passenger below? She must go to him.

"Where is the bilge?" she asked the Chief Engineer.

"Take this lift, Madam," he said, with an admiring glance.

Alone she worked the dangerous electric lift. Alone she groped her way through the roaring hold.

John Tarver saw the light of her lantern flickering among the bales of peanuts.

The ship lurched violently to starboard. Man and woman were flung together with a blinding concussion. Their heads met.

CHAPTER XVIII CROSSING THE BAR

Something snapped in their brains. The veils of oblivion were lifted.

"Husband mine," she cried.

"Wife mine," he said.

THE BATTLE OF THE STEPS

A BRUSH WITH BUREAUCRACY

This is a true story. I am not proud of it, but the painful correspondence reproduced below did actually pass through the penny-halfpenny post. The long battle is now over, and I take up my pen for the help of those who come after.

I live at Hammersmith. My garden wall descends abruptly into the Hammersmith Thames. After the war I decided that I must have, like most of my neighbours, a flight of wooden steps leading from the top of the wall to the foreshore or mud below. It was obviously wrong in principle to live on a great artery and have no means of communicating with it. Also I had acquired a boat, and I wanted to have some way of entering the boat.

So I had a flight of wooden steps constructed, and I painted them green. They were not good steps, and wherever it was possible for the wood to split in the course of construction the wood did split. But I painted them green.

The next day a large motor-boat snorted up to the steps, containing two robust and severe-looking men in blue uniforms and peaked caps. They were officials of the Port of London Authority. Their captain made fast his boat in a seamanlike manner with a round turn and two half-bitches, and gingerly ascended my steps.

I stood defensive on the quarter-deck, and returned his salute.

He was a nice man, with shiny buttons and nautical blue eyes. His name (one will say) was Buff, and let me say at once that my relations with Mr Buff have always been of the friendliest. Many a time he has towed me home in a flat calm, or a gale, or other marine misfortune. He is a good fellow. But he represents Bureaucracy, and, as such, officially I defied him.

He said: "Are these your *steps*, Sir?" in a grave and sinister tone; as one man might say to another, "Is this *your* dynamite?" or "Are these your machine-guns?"

"Yes," I said.

"You've got the Authority's permission, I suppose?" he went on, and it was clear to me that he supposed nothing of the sort.

"Not yet," I said cautiously.

He shook his head reproachfully.

"You mustn't go putting up accommodations on the foreshore without permission of the Authority," he said. "You'll get into trouble." And he looked with menace at my nice green steps, as if for two pins he would tear them to pieces.

"Oh?" I said. "I didn't know." Which was perfectly true, I could hardly have been more surprised if he had told me that the House of Lords were concerned about my steps.

"There's nothing to it," he continued encouragingly. "All you've got to do is to write to the Authority, and send 'em in a plan of the accommodations you require. That's all there is to it. Good-day, Sir." And with a courtly salute he walked down the accommodations, entered his boat, and motored rapidly away.

My wife is an artist. And I asked her to draw a plan of the steps. She drew a delightful pen-and-ink picture of the steps, a vivid, joyous little thing, full of high lights and subtle shadows. Then the correspondence began.

The Man About Town

> "To the Port of London Authority

"SIR,

"I beg to apply for permission to erect a flight of steps (wooden) leading from my garden-wall at the above premises to the River Thames. I enclose a plan.

"Yours faithfully,

"A P HERBERT."

Needless to say, I did not enclose a plan. Some men are born thus. And I, suppose that to the end of my days I shall go on not enclosing things. Alas, how confidently I write, "I enclose so-and-so – I think it will amuse you"; how gaily I lick the envelope and put on the stamp, thinking what fun my correspondent will have over the enclosure; I post the letter, I come in, and I bolt the front door, and I find so-and-so lying on my table; then I sit down wearily and write another letter to say I am sorry I did not enclose so-and-so in the first letter, but I enclose it now; and as often as not I am thinking of something else all the time, and I fail to enclose so-and-so even then. Then I will begin again.

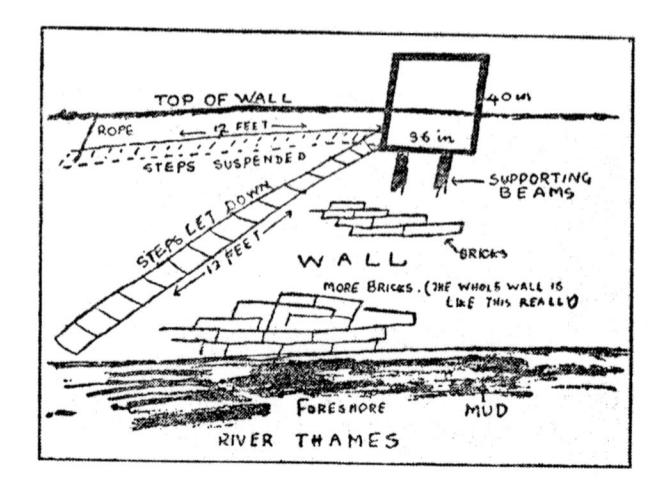

THE STEPS. PLAN (*By me*)
Note the dotted lines showing the position of the steps when suspended.

Generally when a man writes to me and says, "Your three letters of the 15th inst. to hand. We note that you enclose cheque for £3 15s. 1d., but regret to inform you that we find no cheque with either of the three letters," I feel penitent. When the Port of London wrote to say that the plan was missing, I suffered less, for it seemed to me that, plan or no plan, the meaning of my letter was reasonably clear. The plan was surely a mere matter of form. By that time some reckless maid had tidied my wife's sketch out of existence. So in a creative moment I drew a plan myself. It lacked the artistic vigour of my wife's sketch; but no one who studied it intelligently could resist the conclusion that it was intended to represent some wooden steps, of given dimensions, and attached in some manner to a brick wall. I sent it to the PLA, and regarded the incident as closed.

They replied:

"10th May.

"DEAR SIR,

"Referring to your letter of the 25th inst. I duly received the plan enclosed with your letter, but regret that it is not prepared in accordance with the regulations. The forms can be obtained on application.

"Yours faithfully,

"A M BUGGY."

These were the Regulations! like my plan they speak for themselves:

"PORT OF LONDON AUTHORITY
"(River Department)

"REGULATIONS WITH RESPECT TO APPLICATIONS FOR ACCOMMODATIONS IN THE RIVER THAMES.

"Every application for permission to carry out Works upon the banks, or in, upon, under or over the foreshore or bed of the River or adjoining Creeks, should be made upon a printed form and forwarded to the Port of London Authority, River Department, Victoria Embankment, EC. The forms can be obtained on application. Applications must be accompanied by the following *plans in duplicate, at least 20 inches by 15 inches in size*, drawn upon tracing linen, and signed by the applicant:

"I. KEY PLAN. – A key plan prepared from the Ordnance Survey (scale 6 inches to 1 mile), *showing both banks of the River for a distance of at least half a mile above and half a mile below* the site of the proposed works. The position of *the proposed works* should be indicated in red and the applicant's premises coloured in yellow.

"2. GENERAL PLAN. – A general plan of the immediate locality, prepared from the Ordnance Survey (scale – 5 feet to 1 mile) corrected to date when necessary and showing: (*a*) *The proposed works*, drawn in red and coloured red, and the principal dimensions; (*b*) The property of the applicant, coloured in yellow; (c) The *adjoining premises with the names of the owners*; (*d*) The high and low water lines of ordinary tides; (*e*) A scale and a North point. When Ordnance Survey Maps (scale – 5 feet to 1 mile) of the locality are unobtainable, the General Plan should be prepared from the Ordnance Survey (scale 1:2500) and be submitted with a further plan of *the proposed works* drawn to a scale not less than 40 feet to 1 inch, showing the principal dimensions.

"3. CROSS-SECTION. – A cross-section drawn to a scale of not less than $1/16$th of an inch to 1 foot of the part of the foreshore and bed of the river in front of the applicant's premises, with *the proposed works* shown in elevation and coloured red, together with (*a*) Trinity High Water line (*i.e.*, 12 feet 6 inches above Ordnance Datum), (*b*) High and Low Water lines of ordinary tides, and (*c*) the *principal dimensions* of the proposed works. When application is made to embank, the section is to be drawn through the proposed work itself. The surface of every embankment it is proposed to construct within the Metropolitan Area must be at least 5 feet 6 inches above Trinity High Water mark, or 18 feet above Ordnance Datum. When MOORINGS alone are applied for the cross-section will *not* be necessary.

"Any further information with reference to the preparation of the plans will be furnished on application at the office of the Engineer of the Port of London Authority, River Department, Victoria Embankment, EC. The works, if approved, will be assessed in the manner prescribed by Section 116 of the Thames Conservancy Act, 1894, as amended by the Port of London Act, 1908. Works are not allowed to be commenced until the Authority's licence has been executed."

(For the benefit of any reader who has not given his whole mind to these Regulations, I will summarise their requirements:

(1) A Key Plan, prepared from the Ordnance Survey, showing both banks of the river for a distance of at least half a mile above and half a mile below the site of the Proposed Works.
(2) A General Plan, showing, among other things, the adjoining premises, with the names of their owners.
(3) A Cross-Section.
The plans to be drawn in duplicate on tracing-linen, at least 20 inches by 15 inches in size.)

This printed form I took to be an *ultimatum* so monstrous that no State, however small, could with honour accept it. The war had been forced upon me. I would fight.

I replied:

"DEAR SIR,

"I have received your regulations with respect to my application to erect a flight of steps (wooden) on my garden wall, and am arranging to engage the necessary staff of surveyors, architects, draughtsmen, and clerks. It appears to me, however, that the compilation of the required plans will be a lengthy and expensive affair, a little out of proportion, if I may say so, to the dimensions and importance of the proposed works, which, as you will see from the plan I have already sent you, are modest. I understand that there is, at the present time, a rush of business in the surveying world which may make it difficult for some time to secure skilled attention to the matter; and I have neither the time nor the technical training to attend to it myself.

"I write, therefore, to ask if the Authority could on this occasion relax their regulations, which were, no doubt, designed for works of even greater magnitude, and accept a rather less elaborate indication of the nature of my proposed steps.

"Meanwhile, I should be glad if you could return the plan I have sent you, for the purpose of further calculations.

"I am, Sir,

"Yours faithfully,

"A P HERBERT."

The Authority replied:

"26th May, 1919.

"DEAR SIR,
   "*Landing Platform and Steps,
   Hammersmith.*
"Referring to your letter of the 25th inst., the preparation of the plans in this matter is not quite such a formidable process as you apprehend, and I am instructing the Assistant Inspector of the district to call on you at an early opportunity in order to explain what is required.
       "Yours faithfully,
              "A M BUGGY,
              "River Department."

Mr Buff called again in his motor-boat. He was very pleasant.

"These here plans," he said kindly, "you'll have to do them, you know, Sir."

"I know," I said, "I'm hard at it, Mr Buff. I've coloured my property yellow, and I've coloured the proposed works red. I've put in the High Water Line of ordinary tides, and I've found out the name of the man next door. But I can't find Trinity High Water Line. And I can't find Ordnance Datum. What the devil *is* Ordnance Datum, Mr Buff?"

"There's nothing to it," said Mr Buff evasively. "They only want you to give them an idea like."

It crossed my mind that Mr Buff also was unfamiliar with Ordnance Datum: and I delicately forbore to press him. "By the way," I went on, "who does the Island belong to?" (The island is a strip of osiers, reeds, and mud about a hundred yards from my house.)

"The Ecclesiastical Commissioners," said Mr Buff. "Was you thinking of buying it?" he added humorously.

"No," I said, "I was wondering whether I ought to put their names in the plan."

Mr Buff grinned reproachfully and went away.

Two or three weeks went by. Sailing about the river I often passed Mr Buff in his motorboat; and he would trumpet, through his hands: "NICE BREEZE, MR HERBERT. How's THEM PLANS GOING ON, SIR?" And I would cry back across the water: "YES, IT'S A NICE BREEZE, MR BUFF. THEY'RE DOING FINE."

"THEY'RE GETTING A BIT IMPATIENT AT HEADQUARTERS," he shouted down the wind one day.

"YOU TELL THEM NOT TO WORRY," I yelled, sailing away. "I'VE JUST STARTED ON THE CROSS-SECTION. ANOTHER MONTH OR TWO…"

After a few marine conversations of this kind Mr Buff seemed to weary of the theme, though he still referred in kindly terms to the breeze; but I wanted to make it clear that I was taking the plans seriously, and generally had some little problem to put to him about the Scale, or the principal dimensions, or Trinity High Water Line, or what not. One stormy day in the third week I hailed him from afar, and he steamed across to meet me. He stopped his engine, and I raced under his stern, looking worried.

"IT'S ABOUT THOSE PLANS," I bawled, going about and crossing his bows.

"WHAT'S THE TROUBLE NOW, SIR?" yelled Buff his subordinate grinned secretly, and it struck me that Mr Buff was losing interest in the plans.

"IT'S THE OLD TROUBLE," I cried. "THAT ORDNANCE DATUM. I CAN'T FIND IT ANYWHERE. THE WHOLE THING'S HELD UP FOR THAT. CAN'T YOU HELP ME, MR BUFF?" and I bore away on the starboard tack. Mr Buff was to leeward, and the remark he made, though loudly delivered, I was unable to catch; but I fancied it was a cross reference to Ordnance Datum.

After that Mr Buff showed signs of avoiding me upon the waters, and I contented myself with shrugging my shoulders hopelessly when he passed, and peering anxiously over the side, to show that I still pursued the quest. His assistant still grinned cheerfully, but I gathered that to Mr Buff the whole conception of Ordnance Datum had become distasteful. A cruel game, perhaps, but in a battle with bureaucracy all soft scruple must be thrust aside. Only by slashing at its tentacles can you repel an octopus; and only through the tender Buff could I get at that Buggy, the monster

Then one day Mr Buff called again.

"I've brought along Mr Popley's plans," he said. "This'll show you the kind of thing they want."

He unrolled a huge sheet of tracing-linen, and showed me the plan which Mr Popley had submitted when he built *his* steps next door, many years ago. Mr Popley is now dead. But his plans live on. I studied them with reverence.

"There's your Ordnance Datum, you see," said Mr Buff, with some triumph. "Six feet below the river-bed."

"Is that where it is?" I said. "No wonder I missed it. But how exactly does it affect my steps?"

"That's nothing to do with me, Sir," said the honest fellow. "There's the Regulations, and you've got to conform to 'em same as others. Mr Buggy was askin' after you yesterday," he added darkly.

"Dear Buggy," I mused. "Well, Mr Buff, I'm grateful to you. Now that I've had a look at Mr Popley's plans I begin to see daylight."

And that night I wrote to the authority:

"26th June, 1919.

"DEAR SIR,

"I have your letter of the 26th ult., and thank you for sending me Mr Buff, who was of great assistance and kindly showed me the plans submitted by Mr Popley in respect of the steps erected by him next door some years ago. I am straining every nerve to comply with the

Regulations, but meanwhile might, I suggest that in considering my application you might conceivably make use of Mr Popley's plans?

"So far as I know, neither the neighbourhood, nor the bed of the river, nor the High and Low waterline of ordinary tides have materially changed since the date of those plans My proposed steps will be of almost exactly the same dimensions as Mr Popley's steps. My house is the next house to the west of his, and my steps will be at the end of my garden and not at the end of his. My neighbour on the west (No. 13) is a Mr Rumble, who was till lately MP for some part of Scotland, is a bachelor, and takes in the *Nation*; and my neighbour on the east (No 11) is a Mr Fritt, who is an architect and has two grandchildren, if not more. With these exceptions the plans I shall have to submit will be almost identical with Mr Popley's plans, and I venture to suggest that much trouble will be avoided if you simply refer to those plans for the purpose of my application, and a desirable economy will be effected at a time when economy is surely the one hope of this great nation.

"Otherwise I apprehend that the cost of preparing the proposed plans will exceed the cost of erecting the proposed steps

"I am, Sir,

"Yours faithfully,

"A P HERBERT.

He replied:

"28th June, 1919.

"DEAR SIR,

"Referring to your letter of the 26th inst., as you are no doubt aware, the landing platform and steps you have placed at your premises at Hammersmith *can only be allowed to remain* under the licence of the Port Authority, and in order to obtain that licence it is requisite that you should submit the application and plans asked for, and I shall be glad to receive them without further delay.

"Yours faithfully,

"A M BUGGY,
"River Department."

The dog!

In this letter I detected a note of unmistakable menace. In all our previous correspondence there had been observed a decent fiction that my "proposed works" were still in the stage of being "proposed." This was the first time that Mr Buggy had let on that he knew that the proposed works were actually and illegitimately in existence. It seemed to me to be a sinister development, and I own that I was a little intimidated. The proposed steps were being very useful, and though the crusade against tyranny was an end in itself, it was no part of the crusade to have my steps demolished by Mr Buff in a motor-boat. All through that summer the game was to keep the crusade alive, and at the same time to keep the steps intact. And I now felt that the hour of surrender was approaching.

I wrote to Mr Buggy:

"2nd July, 1919.

"DEAR SIR,

"I am pained by the tone of your letter, which wholly ignores what I venture to think was a very reasonable suggestion of mine. However, I must reluctantly bow to your ruling, and hope to be able to submit the required plans within a few days.

"Meanwhile, would you please forward to me the Form of Application mentioned in the first paragraph of your Regulations?

"It is very cold for the time of year.

"Yours faithfully,

"A P HERBERT."

Many of my friends have professed to find something bizarre, if not outrageous, in my concluding remark. I do not understand this. Surely no attempt to humanise official correspondence can be wholly evil. And by this time I felt that my relations with Mr Buggy were taking on a certain intimacy I wanted to reach out to Mr Buggy, I wanted to get at his soul…

From this point matters moved more smoothly. I got an architect to prepare the plans. It cost me a guinea. The architect was a neighbour, or it would have cost me a great deal more. I wish I could reproduce the plans, but they were 20 inches by 15 inches, and it can't be done. They were beautiful plans. The Key Plan dutifully showed both banks of the river for half a mile on either side, not to mention a mile or two of hinterland on either bank. The General Plan was a lovely piece of drawing, every house in Hammersmith Terrace was meticulously distinguished, and you could see quite clearly which of them had conservatories and which of them had only a door into the garden. You could see the reeds on Chiswick Eyot, and there was a beautiful wobbly line, representing the Low Water Mark of ordinary tides, and at the end of my garden was a faint red dot, representing the proposed works.

It took a long time to fill in the Form of Application, but I did it.

This was how it read when duly filled in:

Etcetera

"TO THE PORT OF LONDON AUTHORITY.

(Here fill in name and address of applicant) "I, A P Herbert, Hammersmith Terrace, Hammersmith, W6

do hereby make application for permission to carry out the following works over the River Thames, viz.:

[Here set forth the nature of the works applied for and state precisely for what trade and for what purposes in connection with that trade the works are required.] a flight of wooden steps, painted green, and lead from the wall or boundary of the garden estate or messuage of the above premises to the foreshore bed or bottom of the River Thames for the purpose of the trade of proceeding, from time to time into my sailing dinghy vessel or ship hereinafter called *Leviathan* or the trade, profession, or business of proceeding into the said River Thames to bathe, swim, or paddle as the case may be or the trade, pastime, or occupation of proceeding down the said steps in order to tend, mend, renovate, or clean the good ship *Leviathan* at low tide or simply to walk along the foreshore and take the air *subject to the licence of the Authority mentioned above, to be executed in accordance with the plans which accompany this application.*

"*And I hereby agree to pay the Assessor's fee which, in the event of this application being granted, will be incurred by the Authority in the valuation of the above accommodation under the provisions of the Thames Conservancy Act, 1894, as amended by the Port of London Act, 1908, and also to pay the statutory stamp duty on the deed of Licence or Agreement.*

"Dated this 6th day of July, 1919.

"Signature of Applicant. A P HERBERT.

The Man About Town

"THIS FORM MUST BE SIGNED BY THE APPLICANT HIMSELF AND NOT BY THE ENGINEER, ARCHITECT, OR CONTRACTOR FOR THE WORKS."

I sent in the plans, and I sent in the Form of Application, and in August the Great Permission arrived:

"DEAR SIR,
"Referring to your application of the 7th ultimo, the Port Authority are willing to grant you permission to place a landing platform and steps in front of your premises at Hammersmith as shown on the plan submitted, on condition that the work be carried out to the satisfaction of the Port Authority under the inspection of the Chief Engineer, that it remain during pleasure and be assessed. It is a further condition of the Authority's permission that the steps when not in use shall be hauled up level with the top of the river wall.
"The matter will shortly be referred to the Assessor and I will write you further on receipt of his report.
"Yours faithfully,
"A M BUGGY,
"River Department."

The Assessor is a man of action. He wrote a month later:

"PORT OF LONDON AUTHORITY AND YOURSELF.
"LANDING PLATFORM AND STEPS, HAMMERSMITH.

"DEAR SIR,
"I have been instructed by the above Authority to assess the amount to be paid by you in respect of the above accommodations, and I propose to put this at £1 per annum. Upon hearing from you that you have nothing to

say against this proposed assessment I will report to the Board.
"Yours faithfully,
"R S BROWN."

I replied:
"11 September, 1919.
"ME AND THE PORT OF LONDON AUTHORITY.
"DEAR SIR,
"Thank you for your letter of the 10th inst., *re* the assessment of my proposed accommodations.
"No, I have nothing to say against the proposed assessment of £1. Indeed, in view of the entertainment I have drawn from five months' correspondence about the said accommodations I think it is a very reasonable sum.
"Yours faithfully,
"A P HERBERT."

I wrote one more letter to Mr Buggy:

"DEAR SIR,
"Thank you for your letter of 13th August. In order to remove any outstanding doubts in your mind as to the nature of my proposed works, I enclose herewith a photograph of the proposed works.
"How the days draw in!
"Yours faithfully,
"A P HERBERT."

The real joke in this painful matter is that the Port of London Authority fondly regards itself as free from those hideous habits of Government offices which we broadly describe as bureaucracy (charming word!). And during the debates in 1919 in the House of Commons on the Ways and Communications Bill, which was to put all docks and harbour authorities under

The Man About Town

the Ministry of Transport, a shrill wail went up from the Authority (and the others) at the idea of handing over these business-like and go-ahead concerns to the inelastic, wasteful, and "bureaucratic" methods of a Government Department.

Still, one feels for them. There are men, I suppose, who go about by stealth, seeking to build wharves and piers and such-like accommodations beside the Thames without the Authority's permission; and from that it is a small step to the erection of street factories, fish-markets, and gas-works. That sort of thing has to be knocked on the head somehow; and the Authority, quite rightly, drew up a series of Regulations which should make it so difficult for a man to make a plan of his proposed fish-market, that all but the most determined spirits would abandon the idea of building a fish-market at all. Well and good; but the next thing was that the reckless Mr Popley must begin blocking up the Thames with a flight of wooden steps. Happily, though, there was a weapon ready to hand. There were the Regulations for the Prevention of the Erection of Accommodations by Private Citizens. Obviously in principle there is nothing to choose between a gas-works and a flight of wooden steps; and one form would serve to nip them both in the bud. For most of us, like Mr Popley, are meek and respectable under the tyrant's heel, and will suffer any brutality at the hands of a public, servant. But, now, consider the position of the Authority. It is bad enough that there are a few citizens so obedient and tenacious that they will attain their innocent desires at last by simply doing what they are told. Men like Popley will comply with any Regulations, however monstrous. No form frightens them; and in the end, by sheer docility they force authority to give them what they want – though, fortunately, such citizens are few. But conceive with what merited resentment the Authority must have regarded an obscure Hammersmith ratepayer who not merely took what he wanted, but for seven months, with impertinent mockery, declined to bow the neck! Fool that I was! For at certain stages in our correspondence I indulged in perhaps improper speculations concerning the personality of Mr Buggy, and there were moments when I thought I detected a gleam of humanity struggling to break through the polite austerity of his letters. I even hoped that the matter of my steps might be a welcome interlude of entertainment in the dreary routine of discouraging gas-works; that he a little looked forward to the next letter from the Hammersmith lunatic, and had perhaps a human longing to answer the lunatic in his own vein; and possibly was all the time deliberately provoking me to further flippancy by his unbending severity.

Alas, as I have since heard, I was wrong. Quite wrong. A ray of light and entertainment I did bring into that office; but it was not enjoyed at the top.

Otherwise I might go on. I have added a banister to the Proposed Works, so that the plans are already out-of-date. But the life of a Hampden is a tiring one, and I am not the man I was: I have become respectable like the rest of us. The Battle of the Steps is over, and every year, on the sixth or seventh application, I duly pay a sovereign for them under the Thames Conservancy Act, 1894, as amended by the Port of London Authority Act, 1908. So perishes Liberty in our land.

A few days ago I moored the *Leviathan* about nine feet farther out from the wall: Today Mr Buff called upon me in his motor-boat.

"About your mooring," he said kindly. "You'll have to get the Authority's permission you know, Sir. Just send 'em in a plan – like you did before. There's nothing to it."

"Very well," I said meekly.

ss

A P Herbert

A.P.H. His Life and Times

In 1970 the inimitable A P Herbert turned eighty and celebrated becoming the latest octogenarian by publishing his autobiography. Already much admired and loved for his numerous articles, essays, books, plays, poetry and musicals and his satirical outlook on the world, this time he turns his gaze to his own life and examines the events that brought him to his eightieth birthday – Winchester and Oxford, Gallipoli and France, and then, in 1924, to the staff of *Punch* where he remained for sixty years delighting readers with his regular column.

Alan Herbert was very much an Englishman and a gentleman – outspoken patriot, defender of the good and denouncer of injustice – and, in everything, he retained his sense of fun. And this zest for life that saw him through so much will delight readers as they delve into the life of this great man.

Honeybubble & Co.

Mr Honeybubble proved to be one of A P Herbert's most popular creations and avid readers followed his progress through life in APH's column in *Punch* where he first appeared. Here his exploits are collected together with a cast of other colourful characters from the riches of their creator's imagination. *Honeybubble & Co.* is a delightful series of sketches revealing some of the more humorous aspects of the human nature.

A P Herbert

Light Articles Only

In this amusing collection of articles and essays, A P Herbert ponders the world around him in his own inimitable style. Witty, droll and a respecter of no man, the admirable APH provides a series of hilarious and unique sketches – and gently points the finger at one or two of our own idiosyncrasies. Such comic dexterity and inspired versatility is beautifully enhanced by a string of ingenious illustrations.

Number Nine

Admiral of the Fleet the Earl of Caraway and Stoke is, as one might expect being an Admiral, a man of the sea. In fact, so much so that for him, all the world's a ship, and all the men and women merely sailors…

The Admiral's dedication to King and country could never be questioned – but surely it was a bit much expecting him to give up his ancestral home for the psychological testing of candidates for the Civil Service. Tired of the constant intrusion, and aided and abetted by his son Anthony and the lovely Peach, he embarks upon a battle of wits against the political hopefuls. The result is a hilarious tale of double-crossing, eavesdropping – and total mayhem.

A P Herbert

The Old Flame

Robin Moon finds Phyllis rather a distraction in the Sunday morning service – after all her golden hair does seem to shine rather more brightly than the Angel Gabriel's heavenly locks. His wife, Angela, on the other hand, is more preoccupied with the cavalier Major Trevor than perhaps she should be during the Litany. Relations between the Moons head towards an unhappy crescendo, and when, after an admirable pot-luck Sunday lunch, Robin descends to the depths of mentioning what happened on their honeymoon, the result is inevitable – they must embark on one of their enforced separations. Finding his independence once more, Robin feels free to link up with Phyllis and her friends, and begins to dabble in some far from innocent matchmaking.

This ingenious work brilliantly addresses that oh so perplexing a problem – that of 'the old flame'.

The Thames

A P Herbert lived by the Thames for many years and was a fervent campaigner for its preservation and up-keep. Here, in this beautifully descriptive history, he uses his love and knowledge of the mighty river to tell its story from every aspect – from its dangerous currents to its tranquil inlets, and from its cities and bridges to its people and businesses. Adding his renowned wisdom and wit to his vast knowledge, A P Herbert creates a fascinating and entertaining guided tour of the Thames, and offers his own plans for the river's future. This is the perfect companion for lovers of both London and her waterways.

OTHER TITLES BY A P HERBERT AVAILABLE DIRECT FROM HOUSE OF STRATUS

Quantity		£	$(US)	$(CAN)	€
	A.P.H. HIS LIFE AND TIMES	9.99	16.50	24.95	16.50
	GENERAL CARGO	7.99	12.95	19.95	14.50
	HONEYBUBBLE & CO.	7.99	12.95	19.95	14.50
	THE HOUSE BY THE RIVER	7.99	12.95	19.95	14.50
	LIGHT ARTICLES ONLY	7.99	12.95	19.95	14.50
	LOOK BACK AND LAUGH	7.99	12.95	19.95	14.50
	MADE FOR MAN	7.99	12.95	19.95	14.50
	MILD AND BITTER	7.99	12.95	19.95	14.50
	MORE UNCOMMON LAW	8.99	14.99	22.50	15.00
	NUMBER NINE	7.99	12.95	19.95	14.50
	THE OLD FLAME	7.99	12.95	19.95	14.50
	THE SECRET BATTLE	7.99	12.95	19.95	14.50
	SIP! SWALLOW!	7.99	12.95	19.95	14.50
	THE THAMES	10.99	17.99	26.95	18.00
	TOPSY, MP	7.99	12.95	19.95	14.50
	TOPSY TURVY	7.99	12.95	19.95	14.50
	TRIALS OF TOPSY	7.99	12.95	19.95	14.50
	UNCOMMON LAW	9.99	16.50	24.95	16.50
	THE WATER GIPSIES	8.99	14.99	22.50	15.00
	WHAT A WORD!	7.99	12.95	19.95	14.50

ALL HOUSE OF STRATUS BOOKS ARE AVAILABLE FROM GOOD BOOKSHOPS OR DIRECT FROM THE PUBLISHER:

Internet: www.houseofstratus.com including synopses and features.

Email: sales@houseofstratus.com please quote author, title and credit card details.

Order Line: UK: 0800 169 1780,
USA: 1 800 509 9942
INTERNATIONAL: +44 (0) 20 7494 6400 (UK)
or +01 212 218 7649
(please quote author, title, and credit card details.)

Send to: House of Stratus Sales Department
24c Old Burlington Street
London
W1X 1RL
UK

House of Stratus Inc.
Suite 210
1270 Avenue of the Americas
New York • NY 10020
USA

PAYMENT

Please tick currency you wish to use:

☐ £ (Sterling)   ☐ $ (US)   ☐ $ (CAN)   ☐ € (Euros)

Allow for shipping costs charged per order plus an amount per book as set out in the tables below:

CURRENCY/DESTINATION

	£(Sterling)	$(US)	$(CAN)	€(Euros)
Cost per order				
UK	1.50	2.25	3.50	2.50
Europe	3.00	4.50	6.75	5.00
North America	3.00	3.50	5.25	5.00
Rest of World	3.00	4.50	6.75	5.00
Additional cost per book				
UK	0.50	0.75	1.15	0.85
Europe	1.00	1.50	2.25	1.70
North America	1.00	1.00	1.50	1.70
Rest of World	1.50	2.25	3.50	3.00

PLEASE SEND CHEQUE OR INTERNATIONAL MONEY ORDER.
payable to: STRATUS HOLDINGS plc or HOUSE OF STRATUS INC. or card payment as indicated

STERLING EXAMPLE

Cost of book(s):..................... Example: 3 x books at £6.99 each: £20.97
Cost of order: .... Example: £1.50 (Delivery to UK address)
Additional cost per book:............... Example: 3 x £0.50: £1.50
Order total including shipping:........... Example: £23.97

VISA, MASTERCARD, SWITCH, AMEX:
☐☐☐☐ ☐☐☐☐ ☐☐☐☐ ☐☐☐☐

Issue number (Switch only):
☐☐☐

Start Date: Expiry Date:
☐☐/☐☐   ☐☐/☐☐

Signature: _____

NAME: _____

ADDRESS: _____

COUNTRY: _____

ZIP/POSTCODE: _____

Please allow 28 days for delivery. Despatch normally within 48 hours.

Prices subject to change without notice.
Please tick box if you do not wish to receive any additional information. ☐

House of Stratus publishes many other titles in this genre; please check our website (**www.houseofstratus.com**) for more details.